D1602919

Unexpected Surprise

Sarah J. Brooks

Sarah J. Brooks

ISBN: 9781697240405

Copyright © 2019 Sarah J. Brooks

Author's note: This is a work of fiction. Some of the names and geographical locations in this book are products of the author's imagination, and do not necessarily correspond with reality.

For my readers

TABLE OF CONTENTS

Chapter 1

Sinclair

There was a time when I loved going to movie screenings. I lived for them. I didn't really have as much enthusiasm for the one-hundredth screening of our most successful film, The Dark One. I'd seen it so many times I could recite the entire movie as a one-man show. This particular showing was a special sunset screening on Halloween with a producer's Q & A afterward. I had to go. The sunset timing was important. Our marketing department had timed all the promotions at sunset because that's when the Dark Ones would emerge from the sky. It added an element of scary to all things Dark One.

"They always come just before the night when the sun retreats safely behind the horizon, leaving the rest of us out here on our own… their prey," a girl's voice-over grips us as winged creatures fly down from the heavens.

On-screen dark-winged figures fly out of the dimly lit sky and descend onto the streets of New York City. "They'd come before. I'd seen them in my nightmares," the woman's voice continues as one very large black-winged creature approaches her.

A heavily armed stranger stops in front of the woman and bears his weapons. "Don't you touch her you filthy flying worm!" the man with thickly corded muscles and deep brown skin yells out to the creature.

The woman dips back into his shadow as the hulking man brandishes a machete he unsheathes from a leather holster at his back. The dark angel steps towards him. "Out of my way, maggot."

Without any response, the muscled man stabs at the dark angel with valiant intent. The fallen angel merely waves his hand, and the machete flies out of the man's hand and out of sight.

Undaunted, the man has an arsenal of sharp implements strung about his body. He dislodges a knife and wields it with fervor as he dodges and moves around the angel kicking his kneecaps inward to throw him off balance. The angel curls his long pale fingers around the man's throat. Squeezing with little effort, the man's eyes bulge from his face. His tongue gapes, and he gasps for air. The knife drops from his hand as his body goes limp.

The angel's face stays peaceful, a complete juxtaposition to the horror he's just inflicted. He slowly takes a step towards the girl shivering in the shadows.

"These streets are dangerous," the dark angel growls, his voice deep and husky. "You should be inside, locked up. Don't you know there's a war?" He laughs, making her nervous as he continues to approach.

"Leave me alone!" she screams as she throws punches at the angel's bare chest...

"GO! GO! Girl go with him. He's gonna give you the best sex you've ever had... toe-curling good," a woman shouts from the audience.

Her outburst is met with snickers and words of agreement.

"And his fine ass is going to save the world!" another woman chimes in.

Obviously, a few people at the Halloween screening had seen the film several times. They were right. Among the fallen angels, the Dark One is their vigilante justice, trying to keep them from obliterating humans. He has a band of followers who are trying to petition God to let some of them back into heaven for the good they've done for humanity.

The lady in the audience is right; he is going to give her a night of unbridled pleasure. He'll give her so much pleasure; in fact, the film initially had an NC-17 rating. We had to trim a few thrusts and cut away just before any male genitalia was revealed to get an R instead. I didn't want to limit the film's sexuality. Dante, the fallen angel, was going to be one of the sexiest heroes in action film history. The character straddled the line between good and evil in such a provocative and alluring way that he was already becoming a cult figure.

All in all, the film was a controversial success. It garnered pretty high box office returns and decent critical acclaim. It was the first film of its kind to make an impact on the film industry and finally put my production company on the map.

While I was already a multi-millionaire thanks to a trust fund my oil-rich grandfather had set up for me, I wanted to make my own money. I invested some of my trust funds into the company, which was just starting to turn a sizable profit after the success of the Dark One.

We were working on a sequel. The writer had a lot of mediocre ideas he was throwing around, but nothing was clicking with me yet. We needed to create a great next chapter for the Dark One saga. I wasn't worried about finding a story, even if it meant discovering a new writer. He had let fame go to his head. He wasn't working with the same passion he once had now that he was fielding six-figure deals for multiple projects. I was ready to move on.

At the question and answer session with the audience, I answered several young women's questions about Dragon Kensington, the film's sexy star. Unfortunately, he wasn't there because he'd conveniently come down with the flu. After an hour of answering questions I'd answered a million times before, I promised the sequel was in the works. I then signed a few autographs and had a couple of conversations with aspiring filmmakers. I made it home in time to get ready for the hottest Halloween party of the season.

My brother Sage, who was in the music industry, was able to get us invites. It promised to be a fun time with women, gourmet food, and discretion for those looking for a bit more of a rollicking good time. I was up for some noncommittal sex on occasion and tonight seemed right for it. Unfortunately, my older brother Shelton had also been invited by his law firm. He was the Shady Lawyer to the stars, so I guess he was there to cover tracks for anyone wanting to keep their missteps that evening a secret. Whatever the reason, he was deplorable at best. I was sure to avoid him and stay with my younger, cooler brother. Everyone who was anyone was going to be there, so it was the perfect time to promote my production company.

Chapter 2

Reyna

I could've kissed my roommates Charlynn and Melody for agreeing to go with me to the Hollywood Haunted Mansion party. I was a temp working for the most notorious beast boss on the planet. There was no producer in Hollywood more lecherous or vile. A job was a job, though, and his company was the best indie production company in the industry. If I wanted an in to get my scripts read by people who could actually help me get them produced, I had to work for the best. Even if Regent Pictures didn't pick up one of my films, an employee at the company would definitely know someone.

It took months before I was hired to work for Christopher Regent, even as a temp. I almost died when Chris told me I had to be his plus one for the evening. I assumed it was because we were going to be working. Several well-known actors, actresses, and writers were attending, and I knew he had a list of people he wanted to approach.

I refused to go. It shocked him, but he wasn't surprised. He'd tried to invite me to dinner a few times, and I refused him then as well. He finally told me it was just a party, and I could bring some girlfriends along if I didn't trust him.

"I don't trust you," I flirted, knowing this was the only way Christopher Regent would ever listen to a word I said.

"Why not? I've been nothing but a gentleman." The lechy gleam in his eye said differently.

"Chris, I have a life," I complained as he followed me out to my cube with the invitations in hand.

"You shouldn't. You work for me. It's well known that anyone who works for me doesn't have a life outside of Regency Pictures. Besides, don't you have a film you want to get made? Or are you an actress? I forgot." He seriously was that heartless.

"I'm not going," I turned around and told him flatly. "It's Friday night, and I've already been at work for eleven hours. You've had enough of me for one day." I stood my ground as I grabbed my coat and prepared to leave the office.

"Truce," he cooed, blocking my exit. "My offer stands; I'll let you bring a few girlfriends along. No men, though; this isn't the kind of party that needs more men. Scantily dressed women are always welcome." His eyes glazed over with sick carnal desire.

"My friends don't work for you," I teased, trying to keep this light or I'd lose my job.

While I mostly hated working for Chris, it did put me in contact with people who read my screenplays, and it was good for my resume. Anyone in the industry knew if you could survive a year under Christopher Regent, you were Hollywood gold.

"Yet…" was all he said as he angled in closer.

"Okay. I'll go, but only if I can bring my friends and leave with them when we're ready to go." I couldn't believe I was actually negotiating with him.

I bartered with him because I had to make a solid escape plan. I didn't want to end up in his bed. He was an expert negotiator. Our banter was meant to define for him exactly what he wanted… and I countered with what he'd actually get.

"You'll go with me and leave with me, or you might not come back to work on Monday." His lightly veiled threat sent an icy shiver down my spine as his fingers caressed the cool metal frame of my cubicle.

He wasn't an ugly man; in fact, he was quite handsome for someone in his fifties. It was just his abysmal reputation for having sex with starlets and wannabees that made him repugnant. He also was rumored to use force. He was a demanding man who cared little for others. Combine that with a near predatory sexual pursuit, and you had one vile little man. If enough women dared to stand up to him, he would fall like a deck of cards. But not enough did. So far.

"Really? You're going to fire me? Just because I won't have sex with you tonight? That doesn't work anymore, or haven't you been paying attention to the "Me Too" movement?" I had to just get it out there since this was what we were really discussing.

"I didn't say anything about sex. You read too many tabloids. I want you to stay at the party until I leave, then I'll take you home. I have to make sure we don't let business slip through our fingers tonight. If you stray, you might blabber to the wrong people and lose us a deal. If the bidding war for Carmine's Jungle goes up on the down-low tonight, say for example. You talking to someone about it will ruin my chance of getting the script at its rock bottom price." His smile was smarmy and weak.

I pushed him aside as I made my way out of the cube. "I'm not an idiot. I know not to blabber about deals. Sheesh. It's a surprise you even know my name; you're so clueless sometimes."

He grabbed my arm. "Even still. I'll take you home." His smile was genuine, but it sounded like a threat.

"You promise you'll take me home and that's it." I could see there was no way out of it other than to agree and hope to escape him later. "And my friends can come along and rescue me if I need it."

He laughed heartily. "I hardly think you'll want or need rescuing tonight my dear. This is business." Again, he gave me a warm smile, and I believed him as he released my arm and let me pass.

"Fine." I threw my head back in surrender.

"I'll pick you up at your apartment…" and before he could say more, I interrupted him.

"I'll leave when you leave, but since I'm going with my roommates, they'll take me." I knew it was a long shot, but I took it.

"Nope," he said, writing something on the invitation. "How many of them are you inviting?"

"Two." I looked down at what he was writing.

Please add these two guests to my list… he wrote.

"Names?" He was suddenly very businesslike; short and gruff.

I much preferred this to the murky blurred line between business and pleasure he often liked to cross.

"Charlynn Reeves and Melody Chambers," I answered.

"Sound like porn stars," he said, not looking up from the invitation.

"Shut up," I huffed as I punched him hard on the shoulder.

"Do that again, young lady and I'll reconsider our terms." His face smoldered, and his disgusting smirk was back.

"Just be nice. They have lovely names. You just watch too much porn," I scolded as I crossed my arms over my breasts; a protective reflex.

He laughed. "I don't have to," he said as he handed me the invite. "Give this to your roommates, and I'll pick you up in one hour. Look spectacular. The press will be there." With that, he turned and walked into his office without saying another word.

Our conversations always left me feeling so scrambled. I hoped I'd held my own and didn't unwittingly agree to something I'd regret.

I called the girls from the car as I drove home and told them about the party. They were pretty excited to go because it was going to be the A-list party of the year. If they wanted to meet someone famous, tonight was going to be their chance.

I'd known Melody and Charlynn since we were roommates in college. We were all in our late twenties. Melody was a budding musician whose mother named her Melody because she wanted her to be a singer. Sure enough, that's what Melody ended up being really good at. Charlynn was an architect working for a small firm. She was nuts for sustainable development and using recycled materials. Her designs were pretty cool. They were both the kind of people who would fit right into a high profile Hollywood party: gorgeous, smart, and captivating.

"It says here it's a costume party. I hope I have something to wear," Melody said, with a concerned tone in her voice.

"Wait, we have those Cosplay outfits from Comicon we can wear. Sailor Moon is still pretty in; we can make those work," Charlynn said, jumping off the couch. "This is going to be off the chain!"

I was glad she was excited. I was battling butterflies in my stomach, which had turned into toddler-sized rodents with knives. I seriously thought I was going to throw up.

"You should wear yours too, Reyna," Melody chirped with enthusiasm.

"I was thinking of the Fallen Angel costume I wore last year. It has a mask, so um… maybe Christopher will lose interest? The cosplay thing is too sexy." I was hoping the mask would deter his attraction to me.

"Girl, that dark angel dress, though… your body is on fire in that thing," Charlynn reminded me.

"Yeah, but the mask, the big awkward wings… weapons, you know." I hoped.

"Go with the sexy dark angel. Your Sailor Moon shows too much of your boobs," Melody added.

"Girl, that outfit, though… you sure?" Charlynn cautioned.

"I'm sure. I'll wear a jacket over it." I smiled at her. I knew what she was talking about. The outfit was a bit revealing in places.

"Like a jacket's gonna do it, but okay," she threw out as she walked into her room to get ready.

"What does she mean by that?" I looked at Melody, confused.

"She said your Fallen Angel outfit is hot as fuck. Be careful." With that, Melody also retreated.

Within the hour, we were all ready to go. The girls were going to take Melody's car, which was big enough to fit all three of us in case we had to make a fast escape. We'd made a pact—if Chris did anything weird, they'd whisk me away. If he didn't, and I gave them the thumbs up or texted them I was okay to go; they'd let Chris take me home.

I felt better having them there. I could do this. I knew I could. At least that's what I told myself when Chris showed up at our door.

"Holy fuck, Reyna. That's one hell of a costume," he immediately said as I opened the door.

Dammit, I should have gone with the Sailor Moon or a bedsheet and been a ghost.

"So's that," I said, trying to divert the attention away from me.

He was wearing a devil costume. He had on a black tuxedo with a blood-red tie, red patent-leather shoes, and red horns.

"It's my go-to Halloween costume. Are you ready? Traffic's a bitch. I need to make some calls on the way." He was his usual gruff, demanding self.

I much preferred his horrible gruff demeanor to his lecherous one, so I felt uneasy but okay. "Ready as I'll ever be," I said, turning back and giving the girls a grimace.

Melody laughed, and Charlynn held up her phone as if to remind me I had a weapon. I nodded, and we were off.

Chapter 3

Sinclair

We arrived at the party, and as expected it was full of some of the most beautiful women I'd ever seen. Sage looked a bit overwhelmed, but I was right in my element. The mansion was huge, and people were littered all over the voluminous space. Some were talking in groups; others sequestered in pairs. Most of the women were wearing such revealing costumes they left absolutely nothing to the imagination. The entire place had a sexual vibe to it. There were even people tucked in corners so close to doing it… they might as well have been putting on a show. Plenty of people stood by and watched, lying in wait. It was insane. Sex hung in the air like a heavy, heady musk.

"Let's get drinks," I suggested, pushing us through the clamor of bodies to the bar.

These things always had an open bar. We'd be getting a lot of top-shelf booze. I wasn't a cheapskate by any means. I liked to buy the best and didn't even mind the price, but I also liked getting something for nothing.

"Yeah, drinks are a must." My brother definitely looked like he needed some liquid courage.

"Do you see Shelton anywhere?" I asked, leery of my older brother.

"Ugh, let's hope he's already found someone," my younger brother said, rolling his eyes.

We get two Grey Goose martinis and head out into the throng.

"I can't believe you raided the costume shop for that," my brother commented with a note of disgust.

"It was our highest-grossing film. I'm a walking billboard," I joked. Being blatant was the best way to avoid embarrassment, in my opinion.

The costume wasn't much. It consisted of a pair of black leather pants, a massive set of black feathered wings I was having a hard time negotiating through the crowd, and nothing else. Thank God I hit the gym four days a week. My well-toned body was very much on display. I was grateful for the costume department's suggestion that the Dark One, Fallen Angel Dante, wear a mask throughout most of the movie.

The real reason we had to write the mask into the film was that Dragon, the film's star, had a bad bout of forehead acne we couldn't clear up. So, we added a few lines about his hiding his identity from his father, God, who had thrown him down from heaven on a whim. He wore the mask, and when he was revealed, his father let him back into heaven for being a hero. Who knew a little adult acne would give us a golden plotline. For me, I was grateful because it concealed my face, so I could enjoy being exotic and alluring.

I figured I'd put on a jacket and take off the wings at some point. I wanted to make a grand entrance, though, and I did. My brother was very good looking. In fact, he was the one who looked most like my mom, which meant he had refined, slightly feminine features. His looks gave him a sort of fragility Shelton and I lacked. Sage was wearing a cowboy outfit that, minus the big hat, looked like clothes he would wear on any other day.

Most of the men in the crowd were wearing costumes like Sage's; unassuming and subdued. I had a moment's regret wearing such an outrageous outfit, but it garnered attention and recognition. Most knew I was the Dark One, and so when I doffed the costume to reveal I was the producer of the film, the conversation would come easily. This, at least, was my plan. That is, it was my plan until I saw her…

It was only a glimpse, but what I saw viciously gripped my heart. She was also dressed as a fallen angel. In the places where I'd bared my skin, she had on a silky black dress. Its soft material was so buttery it danced over her bra-less nipples and screamed: "sex siren" from across the room. She had medium sized pert breasts, small enough to go without a bra, but of enough size to be a nice full-handed grope. Her raven hair fell loosely down her back, and her body was so bangin' it would probably make a man cum, just looking at it. God, her curves were everything. Her wings were almost as big as mine, poor thing. I hoped she hadn't smacked into as many people as I had already. She was with Christopher Regent, dressed appropriately as a devil, but wasn't draped on his arm; encouraging.

I saw her only for an instant before she was lost back into the throng. A man wearing a nice suit and carrying a tray approached Sage and me as we were making our way into the party from the bar.

"Sinclair and Sage Harris," the man announced, his face was kind and welcoming. On his tray, he had a few dozen golden keys.

"Yes." I looked down at the tray of keys. "Oh, we're good. We took an Uber," I said to the man apparently collecting car keys; weird they were all single gold ones.

He laughed in a somewhat condescending manner. "No, no. I'm Gerald Raymond; this is my shindig."

I was only a little embarrassed. "Right, Gerald, so sorry." I lifted my mask. "I've only spoken to you on the phone." I reached out my hand to shake his.

My brother, being slightly cooler, didn't shake his hand. "What's up brother?" he asked as he leaned in for a solid bro-hug.

"I'm good Sage… waiting for your new album. My wife is an obsessed fan," Gerald confessed as my brother puffed up a bit with pride.

"I'll send you guys our new album. I've got an mp4 on my computer." Sage was casual and cool speaking about an album he and his band The Grind, had been working on day and night for nine months.

"She'll die. Glad you got some drinks. The bar is open all night. Also, you're welcome to take one of these keys. Try not to lose it, but if you do… well, we have our way of sorting things out. We've got the mansion until Sunday morning, so these keys are for rooms. The room number is on the key. Take one if you want to use it. The mansion has thirty bedrooms; it's practically a hotel, so we have plenty. If you don't need it, well … you should have brought a girlfriend along. You can crash there if you want, but we've completely stocked the rooms for gratifying nights of nocturnal play." He smiled a lustful smile. "If you don't find yourself needing a room, just drop the key in the glass dish on your way out. If you stay, cocktails and brunch will be served in the morning. Either in your room or the dining room."

With that, he handed each of us a key.

"Seriously, Gerald, you throw the biggest ragers!" Sage had a hard time hiding his awe.

"All in good fun." Gerald's face was beaming with pride.

"This is awesome. Thanks," I said as I took the key and

put it in the pocket of my leather pants.

"I hope you make full use of it." Gerald winked. "Gotta make the rounds, just grab a server if you need anything at all. We've got everything you might want."

"Thanks," my brother and I managed to say at the same time; it was almost awkward, but not.

He dangled his key in front of me. "I am so using this tonight." His eyes glazed over with rabid desire.

"Let you out of a long-term relationship and look at you go," I teased.

I hoped it wasn't too soon. Amelia was the love of his life, but she dumped him because he hadn't asked her to marry him. Together for five years and he couldn't pop the question; something was weird about that. He shot me an unamused glare.

"At least I'm not here with a big fucking pair of wings pretending I'm the hottest character in action film history." Touché, he got his dig in.

"Truce." I threw up my arms; he smiled. "Well, I plan on using it." I tapped my pocket. "On her." I nodded my head to the dark angel accompanying Christopher Regent.

My brother laughed at me as he knocked on my elbow.

"I'm going to mingle." His voice was eager, now seeing that I'd cast my line, he wanted to go explore.

"Yeah, right, have fun." I nodded to him, and he moved away toward someone who wasn't going to embarrass him as badly as I was about to. I was leery my other brother might ooze in at any moment, but this opportunity was too good to pass; the girl was too incredible to miss.

The foyer was two stories tall, bookended by two sweeping staircases; very dramatic. It made for an incredible first impression as she approached. For a moment, I thought she was coming for me, but she veered towards the bar. Behind her, hot on her heels was that scoundrel Christopher Regent. As she passed, she saw we were wearing similar costumes. A glorious smile crossed her face, one Christopher Regent didn't miss.

"There you are," I said in a stern and commanding tone as I stepped in front of them, hoping to stop the beautiful dark angel in her tracks.

"Me?" The woman looked around her as Christopher sided up and linked his arm around hers. He was a total prick, a wave of hatred coursed through my veins.

"Yes." I stepped in closer.

"She's with me." Christopher muscled in.

"No, I'm not," the woman said, incensed.

"I like your outfit." I gently stroked her wings, casual and seductive. "I think I might know you from somewhere. Heaven perhaps?" My lips pursed seductively.

"Seriously?" Christopher huffed.

"Or maybe hell?" She rolled her eyes, and we both laughed.

"That must be the place." I knew we were being totally cheesy, but it was glorious.

"Back off buddy, she's mine," Christopher growled.

The girl was not impressed. "No, I'm not." She nearly hit him.

"Hell... Hello? That's my domain." He flared his hand along with his devil costume. "Besides, who the fuck prances around a party without his shirt on? Grow up." Christopher angled the woman away from me as he attempted to whisk her away.

She planted her foot on the ground and wasn't budging. "Go ahead and get a drink, Chris. I'll stay here until you get back," she said, making her intentions known.

"I brought you to this party. You'll stay with me," he cautioned her like a child.

"I'm your assistant, not your slave," she said, her thick red lips looking glossy as the dim light reflected on her mask.

I felt my cock stir. She was a picture of beauty with just enough sexuality mixed with a dash of innocence. She wasn't being lewd or tawdry with my flirtations, but rather sweet and playful. She'd already stayed her ground, and I wanted to nail this deal down.

"I'm dressed as the Dark One." My tone had the stern command of a successful businessman. "It's my film. You may have heard of it," I said as I flashed him a disingenuous smile.

"Right, yes. Very successful little horror flick. What'd that gross you?" Christopher's interest had now peaked.

"About a hundred mil give or take." My tone was casual; my body relaxed as if gross box office on all of our films was that high.

In truth, we'd struggled until the Dark One's success. Now we had a franchise that would put us on the map. Christopher knew this, knew the film would only make us more and more money, and eventually become a cult classic. He'd be stupid not to get in on the ground floor of this franchise. He pulled a card out of his wallet, which he'd retrieved from his back pocket, and handed it to me.

"Call me if something else comes down the pipeline. Or you're interested in blowing this franchise up," he said in a cold and calculating tone. "I'll leave my assistant in your hands for a moment. Perhaps you can pitch her a few projects. She knows our company's taste," he said as he slapped her ass, which jettisoned her forward ever so slightly.

She took a deep breath, and her lips became a thin flat line. "Right," was all she gave him in a respectful but curt tone of voice.

"I'll be right back then," Christopher said. He kissed her neck as his hand brushed across her nipple, giving it a hard squeeze. "When I do, we'll find which room this key belongs to." Her eyes narrowed as he turned away from her and headed toward the bar.

"I wonder why he capitulated and let you stay with me," I said gently, not wanting to scare her. Her boss seemed scary enough.

"He smelled like money." As soon as Christopher was out of sight, her face relaxed. "Horror isn't really my thing, though." She smiled, "But it's Christopher's thing; he's pretty horrible."

We both burst into laughter.

"Do you want to go to a room with him?" I worried she might be obligated to do whatever he asked of her.

"I'm here to work. Going to a room with him is NOT in my job description." Her face fell as stress flattened her lips into a line.

I wished I could see the whole of her face. I could only imagine it was completely gorgeous. The rest of her certainly was heavenly. Her being masked was supposed to be part of the fun and attraction of the evening, but all I wanted to do was rip the damn thing off her face and kiss every part of her.

Chapter 4

Reyna

My plans to ditch Chris and hang out with my roommates seemed completely out of the question now that Chris was determined to get me into a room. I didn't think his threat was real. He wouldn't jeopardize his already sketchy reputation on a temp employee. Also, we'd barely just arrived. Surely, he had more networking to do. No, the threat was simply for the gorgeous masked man's benefit. I'm sure Chris wanted to shuttle me off somewhere away from him, as he seemed to show interest in me. I doubted he would even bring the room up again. At least, I hoped he wouldn't.

I loved talking to the gorgeous masked man before me, but he was a little intense. I needed a break from all the sexual man energy swirling around the room. As much as I wanted to stay and talk to Masked McDreamy, I also wanted to find my roommates. I looked around the room and found them pretty easily. Charlynn was with a group of people who seemed to be enthralled with whatever she was saying, and Melody was jamming in the corner with some other musicians. I could probably sneak into either of their groups of admirers, but it wouldn't be enough to fully ditch Chris. Surely, he'd find me and drag me out again.

At that moment, my only real hope of escape was the sexy stranger. I looked at his hard-muscled body, so perfect. While only part of his face was revealed, the half that showed was incredibly hot. Strong sculpted jaw, soft lips, a sharp but perfectly formed nose, an incredible shadow of stubble dusting his face. I fixated on his lips as he spoke.

He was laughing. I'd just emphatically announced I wasn't Chris' whore in a veiled, but succinct way.

"Reputation has it Christopher Regent doesn't care what's in your job description. If he wants it, he gets it," the masked angel cautioned.

"Not me." I was flirty but firm.

Unfortunately, Chris came back much faster than I expected. He handed me a cold drink. I had no idea what was in it and no intention of actually drinking anything he gave me for fear it was laced.

"It's the house specialty," Chris said after seeing me inspecting the glass with a questioning eye.

"What's in it?" I asked, hoping it wasn't something totally wicked.

"Just drink it," he ordered, sounding irritated. He then looked over to the masked stranger. "You're still here?" Chris turned to me and inquired, "Did he pitch anything good?"

"Well, he couldn't pitch much you were gone all of the forty-eight seconds." I screwed my face into a frown.

"Pays to have clout." He took the key from his pocket again and dangled it in my face. "I've had enough of this party. Come, it's time we see what this key is for." Chris' eyes narrowed into a sinister leer.

"No thanks, I'd rather stay at the party. Since it seems you aren't here to work anymore, I'm going to mingle." I flashed him a plastic smile and took a step away from him.

His arm reached out, and with a vicious grip, he grabbed me back. "The hell you are." His voice was an angry hiss.

"Woah there, buddy. I think I heard her say she wanted to join the party," the masked stranger said as he removed Chris' arm from me with force.

Christopher looked at his hand. "I wouldn't touch me if I was someone who wanted the biggest producer in Hollywood to consider doing business with him." His face morphed an angry scowl.

For that moment, I was grateful I was wearing a mask, so Chris couldn't see my shocked and appalled expression.

"I'm surprised in the "me too" era you'd be so bold as to attempt to force a woman in your employ to join you. We both know what the gold keys are for." The masked man was calm and steady as he jabbed his barb into Chris.

No one ever called Chris out on his shit, most just shut up and put up with it. He'd definitely had his share of scandals, but none ever got farther than the gossip pages. The woman who was his assistant before me was a temp just like I was for two years before Chris hired her on. As a celebration for her new permanent employment, he took her to the apartment he kept near work, the one his wife didn't know about. He bought her flowers, chocolates, champagne, and a box of condoms. She had a boyfriend and kept trying to tell him she wasn't interested in anything "personal." He merely said the job could be just as easily filled by anyone. She told me this just as she left and I took her place at the company.

"He laughed," she told me when she was training me for her job, "and said if I wanted to move up in the company, this was the first step on the ladder."

After that conversation, I realized at some point he would wager my job for sex. She had decided it wasn't worth it to fight against him and spent several nights with Chris at his apartment until he got tired of her.

"He's small and cums fast; it's twenty minutes tops, then a cigarette, a nap, a second round, and you're done," she whispered. "Jobs like this are hard to find. Just to let you know. No one is above it." It felt like a threat.

With that being said, she packed up her things and moved on to the development department where Chris had gotten her a job as a Jr. Development executive.

"Now, I have this sweet gig." This is what her words told me, but her face didn't seem to agree.

From the moment she explained to me what a letch Chris really was, I vowed never to get sucked in. I could get my screenplays produced the legitimate way. I knew I was talented, and it was just a matter of time before someone was ready to take a chance on me. I had to stay strong and confident. Nothing was worth my dignity. I wish the last assistant knew that. I felt sorry for her, even though she claimed she had chosen by her own free will.

"What I do with her in the room is none of your business," Chris said, dragging me away from the "Dark One."

I wrenched my arm away from him. "I'm not going to a room with you."

"This is ridiculous; let's go. Send whatever you've got to my office on Monday," Chris said as he shuttled me away from the sexy, shirtless, angel.

"No, Chris," I smashed my hands into his chest, hoping it hurt. "This is ridiculous. We're obviously done working. You go enjoy the room; do whatever you want in there, and I'll see you on

Monday." I fixed my wings, which had fallen askew, and turned away from Chris.

"If you don't come with me now, you don't have to bother showing up on Monday," Chris hissed.

"Fine." I gave him a big fake smile and continued to walk away.

The sexy dark angel extended his arm to me as I approached. "May I have this dance."

The live band which had been playing ambient music all night had turned up the volume and had started to rock.

"I love this song!" My face brightened; music was just what I needed to relieve my tension and help me forget that I'd just lost my job with the biggest asshole on the planet.

I didn't dare look back to see if Chris was watching us as I took the dark stranger's arm and headed out to join the gaggle of people dancing. When we settled into a spot on the floor, I asked, "Is he still there?" I didn't really want to know, but I was morbidly curious.

"Yep, he's still there. Just watching us dance. He's a real creep, huh?" My masked savior seemed sensible and very aware.

"Yeah, he's a horrible creep." I rolled my eyes, then rolled my hips. "Let's just dance. I was only a temp anyway." I laughed as I threw my head back and just let the music take me away.

"If you lose your job, you'll have a lawsuit on your hands for sure," he said as he grabbed me and twirled me around. I squealed with joy.

His body was beautiful. I did everything in my power not to rake my fingers over his perfectly toned abs. I also wanted to rip his mask off and kiss him wildly and run my fingers through his sandy brown hair. I was never so wanton; in fact, I'd been a bit of a prude most of my life. I'd kissed men, and I loved to flirt, but I rarely got past the kissing. On a few occasions, I'd let my dates finger me to orgasm, but I often left them hanging without giving them so much as a blow job. I didn't do it to hurt them, I just ... I struggled with casual sex.

I didn't have a great reason for this, other than I was afraid. At twenty-eight years old, I'd only had penetrative sex with one man, my high school sweetheart, Emanuel. He and I had dated since we were fourteen. We slept together after prom when I was seventeen and a half. That first time wasn't so amazing; in fact, it was quite awkward for both of us. However, over the next five years, we learned to rock it in the bedroom. He could really make me howl. I thought we'd last. I knew we would, so I didn't really notice when he started drifting away.

It began when he enlisted in the army. I thought I'd die waiting for his first tour of duty to end. It was the worst eighteen months of my life. When he came home, we fucked like bunnies. We had sex morning, noon, and night for six days, and then he lit up a cigarette and stopped talking, laughing, or being him anymore. I asked, begged, and grilled him for reasons why he'd shut down. I tried to do the things we loved together. Go to the Hollywood sign and kiss, watch a movie at the summer outdoor movie theater, bodyboard in the surf of Santa Monica, but none of it really sparked him. I began to wonder what the army had done to his spirit.

Then one day, Daleann Rivers called while he was on the toilet. I answered his phone because the caller had called three times in a row. I thought it was urgent. It turned out the call was urgent for her at least. Emanuel hadn't returned her calls.

"Are you his boss?" I asked, wondering why she made everything sound so desperate.

"Who are you?" she asked, frustrated.

"I'm his girlfriend," I answered innocently.

"The fuck you are!" she screamed. "*I'm* his girlfriend."

My heart fell to the floor. That explained it all. I didn't understand why Emanuel was cheating on me with the angry woman on the phone. I never knew why he thought she was better than me. Maybe because she was new and I was… established. Perhaps it was because our political views were skewing farther east and west, him being more of a conservative and me spreading my liberal wings. Despite our growing differences, we'd talked about marriage before he left for his tour of duty. I was half-expecting him to propose as soon as he got home, not have another girl somewhere else.

I could have fought it, but deep inside, I didn't want to. Ever since he told me he wanted to enlist in the Army, I knew we were on different paths. I was a peace-loving writer with deep heart-felt movies to sell. He was a walking action figure. It was fine when we were young and gangly, but as we grew into adulthood, we drifted away. Despite the rightness of the breakup, it still took me years to get over the loss.

I was proud of myself though because I was having no problem whatsoever risking my job to be with tall, dark, and winged. At least I was cured of my lovesickness… finally.

Chapter 5

Sinclair

The girl had spunk that's for sure. I didn't know many who could hit Christopher Regent and blow him off so easily. It definitely seemed like he was going to make good on his promise to let her go the next day. However, he lingered… or rather, lurked. He watched her dance for a few songs. Her body was poetry in motion. She had a flirty coolness about her and confidence for days. No wonder Regent had his panties in a bunch; he must have thought he was really close to landing the goddess dancing like a dream before me.

Her perky breasts bounced ever so slightly with the beat, the nipples peaked with exertion and hopefully arousal. Sweat clung lightly to her skin, making her thin silk dress slick enough to form over those perfect breasts. I could see they tapered down to a small waist and legs that didn't stop. The woman was tall, lean, and beautifully poised. She must've been a dancer at one point in her life; she was so graceful.

I was tempted to ask her name and take off our masks and get to know her better, but in light of the Christopher thing, I thought it best not to. Revealing ourselves would probably complicate things. Dancing in the middle of the mansion with a jealous uber-producer fuming on the sidelines was too much fun, though. The whole situation had me painfully aroused.

"Gotta hand it to you, you've got that man wrapped around your finger." I laughed, hoping I wasn't being offensive.

She rolled her eyes again. "Really? He's still there? How pathetic."

Knowing Christopher was looking at her, she swept her arms gracefully down my chest, which was a bit moist with perspiration, and slowly gyrated against my body. Oh, she was dangerous. But that did the trick, Christopher stormed off in a huff. I laughed out loud.

"You really don't care if you lose your job?" I asked, my

body gently grinding against hers.

My cock was ready to be liberated from my black leather pants, so I made sure to keep it away from her, lest I give the wrong impression.

"I care that I have a good time." She flashed me a smile that lit up her eyes. "I'm really thirsty. Let's get a drink."

I gently took her hand and navigated her through the crowd to the bar, which was teaming with people. Luckily, my brother was one of them.

"Sage," I yelled out, deftly cutting our way through the line.

Now cutting in line is rude, but in Hollywood, it's all about who you know and who admits knowing you. My brother graciously made space for us, and no one behind us made a stink, so we were that much closer to our goal.

"Having fun?" he asked, seeing my masked twin.

She gave Sage a flirtatious smile and leaned her body a little more into mine.

"We're having a great time." I squeezed the goddess' hand. "You?"

"The jam was awesome." My brother's face lit up like the Fourth of July.

"You guys were amazing. You're getting so good." I meant the compliment; my brother was really finding his groove in the music industry.

He was the lead singer of the Grind and also played lead guitar. Who knew my pimple-faced little brother would turn out to be such a hunky success. People pretty much just melted for him. They melted for me too, but I tended to be mean at times. I was mostly an alpha; however, tonight I was laying back a bit. My brother had his alpha moments for sure. He could command a lot from people but tended to be more peace-loving and kind than I was. Maybe my rough edges were from being a middle kid, who knew.

"That was you singing just now? You really rock… I mean, really." The goddess seemed truly impressed.

It made me a bit jealous as my brother had the looks to steal her out from under me; however, it wasn't his style.

"Thanks," was my brother's humble reply.

"Have you seen Shelton?" I asked, instantly regretting it. I didn't care where Shelton was; it would only bring down my mood if I actually saw him.

"He's slithering about," Sage said as he handed the goddess and me drinks. "These are wicked." He flashed us a devilish smile. "You two be good. I gotta get back to the band."

With that, my brother was off.

"How do you know the band guy?" the masked goddess asked, sipping her drink.

"He's my brother. You wanna dance some more?" I quickly segued away from any more talk of my brother. I couldn't bear her being interested in my brother instead of me.

"Not really. Unless you do." Her face was flushed red, and I could tell she needed to get some air.

"No, we should probably get you some air, you look a little flushed." She was quite red-faced and radiant.

"Yeah, I'm feeling rather hot." She was hot, alright.

Outside, the patio was more crowded than inside. I didn't

want to suggest we go out there. It was so loud inside we could barely talk. So, I dared to be bold for the sake of privacy and considered asking if she wanted us to use my key. I had to be honest; the move was a little underhanded. I definitely wanted to get to know all of her a lot better, and being in a room prepped and ready for the sexual exchange was almost too convenient.

"Don't take this the wrong way, but I have a golden key as well. Maybe we can go to my room just to get away from all of this. We can come back later." I was being a gentleman; at least I was trying. If I were being my true myself, I'd have had her pinned to the wall by now. I was trying a new approach, since fast and furious wasn't really very satisfying in the end.

"Sure, I'd love to get out of here." Her smile was glorious.

Just out of curiosity, I scoped the room once more to see if I could find Christopher lurking. Sure enough, he wasn't far away. What I found most disheartening, however, was the fact that he was with my horrible brother Shelton. I knew Shelton represented his production company, but I bet Christopher was covering his tracks, perhaps realizing he'd sexually harassed his assistant right in front of me.

He knew I was his lawyer's brother. It wouldn't be hard to find out who my gorgeous companion was; however, I liked leaving it a mystery. Seeing her as a masked goddess added to the sex appeal of the evening. Leaving my mask on allowed me to be the Dark One and not dominant, work-obsessed Sinclair Harris, the indie producer on the rise. If I discovered, through our mutual contacts, that she'd lost her job, I'd assist her in getting another one. I'd see him brought down, even if his lawyer was my older brother.

Luckily, I was able to sneak my winged companion away without being noticed. It was nearly impossible because both of us were wearing massive wings, but with the noise, dancing, and other partygoers wearing gory costumes, we were able to dart to the elevators without being seen.

Once inside the small elevator, we both laughed as our wings hardly fit. We had to position ourselves in such an odd way we were craning our necks at uncomfortable angles trying not to spill our drinks. It made for a funny picture and a nice moment of levity. She was someone I desperately wanted to fuck. In fact, stripping that tiny silk dress off her body was all I could think about. I tried to focus on her mouth or other things, but my eyes kept going to her tits and farther down to the apex of her thighs where the dress material naturally dipped inwards. I had to actually hold my hands so they wouldn't feel her sweet ass sloping elegantly behind her. I had to keep telling myself we were just going to the room to talk, just conversation, no fucking… oh, I was so screwed.

I was greatly relieved when the elevator doors opened, not just because I was truly uncomfortable, but her nearness caused my erection to double in size. Already it was jutting out behind the soft leather pants. I wasn't wearing underwear because I worried the low rise waist might show my boxer brief waistband. That, and I liked the feel of the smooth leather on my cock and balls. The pants were outrageously expensive, and so the leather breathed nicely. They felt fucking incredible.

"Whew," she said as she stretched her arms out exiting the elevator. "That was a tight fit." She smiled as she tried to negotiate her wings out of the small space.

"I'll say," I quipped pretending not to be making innuendo in my head. "Okay, room 35?" I looked at the wall and painted in elegant scroll were tiny number groupings.

Our room was to the left.

"The wall says, it's this way," she noted as her eyes lowered ever so slightly, to discover my cock standing straight and proud. "Follow me." She bit her lip, turned, and marched toward our room, seemingly very eager to get there.

Chapter 6

Reyna

I didn't look back at him, but I knew he had the largest hard-on I'd ever seen. We were grinding on each other a lot on the dance floor. His cock hadn't deflated at all, which told me a lot about the direction we might've been heading in.

I couldn't believe I was going through with this. I'd never gone to someone's room. Especially with a man whose face I hadn't even seen. I really wanted to beat myself up for being an idiot, but he was amazing. I had to admit, at least to myself, I was buying the fantasy. Being a writer since I was a little girl, I was a sucker for getting lost in my head.

We walked into a room decorated in modern minimalist furnishings. The decor surprised me because the rest of the mansion was so lavish and old-fashioned. Everything about the night seemed surreal at that point. I knew what I was getting into, and honestly, I couldn't wait to get into it.

"Um," I looked at the beautiful stranger, trying not to focus on his erection. "Should we?" I motioned to my mask, wondering if we should remove them and shatter the fantasy.

He was in the middle of an awkward pose, trying to angle his way out of his massive wings and hide his bulge at the same time. "Well, these are coming off that's for sure." He laughed as he caught himself looking strange and awkward. "But I think the masks should stay." His voice was deep and husky; the sound of it made me tingly all over.

"Oh? Okay, wings off, masks on." I took my wings off

33

with a little more ease as they were much smaller than his.

I'd bought the costume from a high-end masquerade store last year for a huge charity event Charlynn's company had thrown. The outfit was quite expensive, but I'd loved it from the moment I saw it. The dress was especially beautiful. It was simple and elegant, and the fine silk hugged my curves without being too revealing.

"I know it's weird, but I like the anonymity the mask provides. You don't have to stay if you don't want to. You're always free to go anytime you want, but I need to keep the mask on. It's a costume party, after all."

His smile was boyish, but he was making excuses, obviously needing his identity to remain a secret. Either he was a famous actor and didn't want me finding out who he was, or a serial killer and I was going to die. Somehow, none of that scared me. I was ready to dive right into debauchery with a masked stranger I most likely would never know.

"You're not a serial killer, are you?" I half-teased.

"I promise you I'm not." His voice was total seduction. "Are you hungry? They have a room service menu here." He picked up an iPad sitting on the table and glanced it over.

"If you are." Frankly, I wasn't hungry for anything other than him. The low lighting, the woodsy smell, someone had prepared this room for sex, and it was electrifying every nerve in my body.

"I'm not particularly hungry. They have champagne and chocolate strawberries. Those sound nice." His fingers punched the tablet. "I'm ordering some and water." He smiled seductively as he set the tablet aside when he finished. "It should only be a few minutes."

"Sounds perfect." I tried not to seem awkward, but I was uncomfortable as all I wanted to do was kiss him.

I took a sip of my very potent drink, at least giving my hands and mouth something to do. I'm sure he could sense my discomfort as I sat awkwardly on the couch. There was one big overstuffed chair, a king-sized bed, and a couch in the corner in front of a massive television. I opted for the couch, leaving room for us to share.

"Are you uncomfortable?" he asked as he approached me.

"I'm a little fidgety," I confessed, involuntarily screwing my face into a grimace.

"You don't have to be. Nothing is going to happen here tonight that you don't want to happen." He extended his hand to me.

I set my drink down and held his warm hand with my cold one as our palms touched. "That's what I'm afraid of." My eyes cast to the floor as rockets started blasting in my belly. This man was tempting me to be so dangerously naughty. His hand lifted me from the couch as his arm snaked around my waist and drew me in closer. I could feel the strength of his body against mine. Through the thin fiber of my gown, I also could feel the demanding hardness of his cock. Neither of us mentioned his arousal, but there was no denying it.

"Don't be afraid," he whispered in my ear as he moved our bodies to the sound of silence. "Letting go and experiencing pleasure is natural. Anything that happens here tonight will be consensual and anonymous. Let's just give in to the fantasy and play. No strings, no repercussions, just enjoy the moment."

I nestled into his warmth as we danced to the sound of our own heartbeats, his hips rocking against mine. The power of his rigid cock between my legs made me so wet. I knew exactly what he wanted from me, and I wasn't opposed to giving it to him. I undulated on him ever so slightly as my cheek rested against his firm chest. He was almost a foot taller than me, and I felt small, yet surprisingly powerful in his arms. He didn't lord over me as Chris might, but rather enjoyed our nearness. However, as we continued to dance, our bodies built up electrifying friction. My desire for him spiraled into a near frenzy. We were traveling quickly down the rabbit hole, and he knew it.

"Maybe some music would be good right now." He looked at me with a misty expression.

While I couldn't see his face clearly, I knew what he was thinking. Oddly the mask made it easier for me to understand what his eyes were saying. The elaborately decorated eye holes highlighted his beautiful green eyes. They shone like emeralds rimmed by dark satin and gold swirling trim. For a moment, I regretted my muddy brown eyes thinking them uninteresting compared to his bedazzling jeweled ones.

I'd been told over and over again that my dark coloring was magnificent and exotic. My skin was naturally tanned, my eyes and hair were almost black, and I was alluring in a mystical way. Most people said I was so strikingly beautiful it was hard to believe I was real. I never paid much attention to my looks more than grooming and self-care. I didn't buy lavish outfits, nor did I spend a fortune on trying to look good.

I was a natural beauty and happy about it. I never thought though that I'd be so relieved to be wearing a mask as I was that night. Standing there feeling my insides crumple and my pussy melt, I knew all tall, green-eyed, and handsome had to do was barely breathe that he wanted me, and I'd say "yes" to anything. I was almost assured I'd do something I'd come to regret later, so I was happy no one knew who I was. At least I hoped they didn't, but honestly, I was only fooling myself.

"Some music would be lovely," I cooed as he lifted his Apple watch and synced it with the Bluetooth speakers in the room. Suddenly we were surrounded by sound.

The music he chose was perfect for the moment, not too sappy or romantic, but eclectic and jazzy. He rolled his hips on mine to the languid beat. I could feel his cock sliding up and down over the thin silk barrier between us. I wasn't wearing much underneath, intentionally. I wanted to feel sexy and beautiful. I knew I would be attending the party with Christopher that night, so I wanted to feel powerful. I had absolutely no intention of giving myself to him, but since he often let his cock guide his actions, I tempted the Devil. I had only hoped I could keep him at bay. Luckily, Mr. Masked McDreamy showed up instead.

"I never do this," I blurted out like an awkward teenager who just had her first kiss at the prom.

"You wouldn't be so uncomfortable if you did." His voice was a velvet purr. "I promise not to hurt you, and I won't do anything you don't want. If all we do is drink champagne, eat strawberries, and dance, I'm good. You're beautiful. I could just stare at you all night and be the happiest man alive."

"Wow, that would be intensely awkward." I laughed as the music escalated, and I started losing myself to the beat.

"It would be a bit strange as I'm not even going to have the pleasure of seeing all of your beautiful faces." He took my hand and twirled me around, effortlessly. "Yet, it's Halloween night, so let's let fantasy rule… like in the movies."

He was being so sappy that it made me laugh. "How should we go about this? And should I feel strange that I've just ditched one man to fall in the arms of another?" I was being flirty and fun, but I stopped for a moment, being more serious. "I've only been with like... um, not many people." I couldn't tell him how few, but I needed him to know I wasn't a slut. "This is something... I... don't." Ugh, I was so failing at this.

"Human sexuality is dictated by desire. If you want this, it's okay. It's fine to have a physical exchange with someone you have no intentions of marrying or being with forever, or even really knowing. If you want it... exploring your body, your mind, and your desires are fine as long as you feel you always have a choice. I can't tell you who I am, but I can make you feel like a queen for the night. I can pleasure your body in a way that only fantasy can truly rival. Or not... it's your decision." His voice was level and honest, and somehow it made me feel comfortable and safe, something I never felt around Chris.

At that moment, just after his convincing speech, the door knocked.

"Come in," the masked man said as a woman in a long black dress with ruby red lips and a line of blood dripping down them opened the door and wheeled in a cart.

"Where would you like me to put this?" she asked in a sweet voice.

"Just there is fine," he answered, releasing me and approaching her. "Would you like me to sign something?"

"No, everything is on the house." She smiled, gave a little nod, turned, and walked out the door.

"Oh my God, really? Who's throwing this party?" I asked, astonished that someone could afford to pay for everything.

"Someone very generous." He flashed a sultry smile as he

brought white chocolate covered strawberry up to my mouth.

I opened for him feeling just a little strange.

His warm, inviting smile helped ease my discomfort. "I am your prince." His voice lowered, dark and commanding. "You, Goddess, are mine!" He took my hand, brought me closer.

I did everything in my power not to giggle or drool strawberry juice down my face and ruin the whole thing. "You're my what now?" I managed to squeak out after swallowing.

"Play with me," he commanded in a soft, deep tone. "I'm your dark angel, your prince, your lover. I've taken you from the stockades. A goddess enslaved by our mutual enemy. I've just liberated you from captivity."

I couldn't hold it back, I giggled. "Oh my gosh, okay. Let's do this." I stared deep into his eyes as I tried to get my giggles under control.

"I'm not your master," he continued. "You are the one who owns my heart and soul." His hand coursed over the back of my body, resting just above my ass.

His cock jutted out between us, and he was an impressive size from what I could feel, which made me so hot; he was barely going to fit inside of me. His hand traced across my ass, lightly, like a breeze. That's all this sex-starved body needed. My head dropped back, and he kissed the nape of my neck, breathing hotly.

"And I will finally have you tonight."

What the fuck have I gotten myself into?

Chapter 7

Sinclair

I was glad she was willing to play along. From the moment she walked into the room, I had to have her. She was beautiful, sexy, alluring. She had an air of grace about her and was so fucking astounding in that silk dress. Her sexy mask threw me into paranormal fantasy mode. I may have been nearly a millionaire, but at heart, I was still a little film geek. I loved films like Gabriel and the Prophecy. I was someone who could easily get lost in my own head. Despite my desire for fantasy, I also like control, so getting the muse to play along was paramount to the evening's success.

The only way I could tell if she was willing to enjoy a night of pleasure with me was to show her how fun it all could be. After giving her the strawberry, I gently kissed her soft lips, tasting the sweet chocolate on them. Her eyes sparkled. I then released her from my embrace and poured us two glasses of champagne, preferring champagne to the two high octane drinks they'd given us at the bar. Neither of us drank much of them, but the champagne was so nice.

"What should I call you?" she asked, looking a little more interested in playing, as she took a healthy drink from her champagne glass.

"Master," I said with a straight face, even though I was kidding.

"Really?" She seemed to frown, and her mouth broke into a crooked line. "Isn't that a little too Christian Grey? I thought I um… what was it… slave goddess?" She heaved an exasperated sigh.

"You can call me the Dark One." I tried not to laugh; it was a bit much.

"No." She shook her head, laughing. "No. I can't. I wouldn't be able to keep a straight face."

"Bill?" Now we were having fun.

"Absolutely no!" She crossed her hands in front of her, pouting like a child.

"In all honesty, my nickname is Sin. You can call me that," I said as I unwrapped her folded arms and kissed her lips again.

"Sin? You're serious?" She seemed amused.

"Deadly." She was staring at me with her deliciously deep brown eyes.

"Sin it is then, though I find it a bit ironic. Since that's what we are doing." Her voice dropped to a whisper.

"Only if you're a devout Catholic." I needed to keep her focused.

"My nickname is Rey," her gorgeous lips said as they finally broke into a smile.

"Rey. Like a ray of light, my beautiful captive goddess." I lifted my champagne glass to make a toast, and she did the same.

"To Rey and Sin and an evening we'll never forget." I took a sip of my champagne, which was delicious.

She drank hers as well. "And I hope you're not a serial killer." She flashed me a toothy grin.

"I'm not," I breathed as I moved in closer to her again and planted a kiss on her chin. "Shall we enjoy these on the balcony before I ravage you?"

I heard a gasp escape her, and she nodded. Ah, this was going to be fun. It was clear to me she didn't have much experience with this sort of dating. She'd been a bit fidgety but brave all evening. With other women I'd dated, we'd already be naked by now, most likely having post-coital champagne instead of using it as a warm-up. I had to ease her into the evening, going slow, being gentle, which wasn't really my style.

I was an aggressive go-getter. I made things happen. Despite my penchant for fantasy, I was still in charge of every aspect of my world. We walked out onto the terrace to see Hollywood spread out gloriously before us. I slipped up behind her and caressed the sides of her gorgeous thighs as my leather-clad cock saddled up between her ass cheeks. She nervously took another sip of champagne as my hands smoothed around to the front of her dress and stroked her tight, flat stomach. I loved her body. She was well sculpted, yet feminine and soft. Her breathing hitched at my touch… oh to get her under me; I could hardly wait. Since she was so shy, I let the fantasy build as I kissed her shoulder.

"Will you submit to me?"

She giggled as I trailed kisses along her shoulder to her neck. "Will you be gentle with me?" Good, she was getting into this.

"It depends if you behave." I bit her neck as her head tilted back.

"What will you have me do?" she asked as a shiver coursed through her body.

"Just relax," I coaxed her to release herself to the experience and stroked the bare skin on her arms.

I could tell she wasn't quite ready for me, so I sat in one of the large chairs and set her down on my lap. Of course, she was sitting right on my cock, so it was hard not to dive it right into her, but I ignored it as we drank our champagne. The view was incredible and very similar to the one I had from my own mansion. It was smaller than this one, but equally as grand. We gazed upon the city. I held her in my lap and caressed her body tenderly.

"Looking out at a view like this, sometimes I feel so small. That's one of the reasons why I write," she interjected as my hand gently spread her legs so I could stroke her bare skin. "I want to leave something behind, a story people could remember." The glimmer in her eye was too beautiful.

As much as I wanted to lift her onto my cock and fuck her, talking and musing on life felt hypnotic. "I think Hollywood is full of immortals. Some even become legends because their work is remembered and admired forever. Perhaps, Rey, you will be legendary. I know tonight will be emblazoned in my memory." It was cheesy, I know, but I finally gave in to the urges I could no longer suppress. "You've finished your champagne. Do you think I might ravage you now, Goddess?" I couldn't take much more of her sitting on my cock.

It had been waiting all night for this.

She turned to me and kissed my lips. I obediently opened my mouth for her and slid her dress up over her ass, finally touching its soft roundness.

Her lips parted from mine momentarily as she breathed, "Be gentle."

It was all I needed. I lifted her into my arms, bridal style, and carried her into the room. As soon as I laid her on the bed, I laid beside her and reclaimed her mouth. My tongue slid along the sweet soft part of her lips and begged entrance, which she granted, softly panting. I slid in, thrusting gently, tasting her as my hands, which had been relatively chaste, became more ardent, lifting her dress over her head, leaving her in only a pair of lace underwear. My hands slid along her soft velvet skin to find her bare breasts. At the touch of my warm hands, she drew in a deep breath, and a soft moan escaped her mouth into mine.

My fingers danced over a nipple, feeling it rise between my fingers as she arched in closer. I met her body with my own, now moving my aching cock against her, grinding in hard. Our rhythm, slow and sensuous, built to a frenzy.

"You're magnificent," I breathed as my hand found her aroused nipple.

I gently pinched the peaked flesh as she yelped. "Sin, what are you doing?"

"I'm attending you, my goddess. Since I've liberated you from slavery, now I'll feast." I kept my voice steady as I gently nibbled at her breast.

Her skin flushed as goosebumps covered her body. When one nipple was fully aroused, I slid over the other and nibbled at it. Satisfied I'd gotten their attention, I continued to kiss her rosy pink areola while scooping the soft mound of her breast into my mouth. I supped on the tiny bud as it grew more turgid. With my other hand, I pinched and soothed over her neglected nipple while her pussy warmed my rigid cock.

I stopped sucking on her to command, "Touch me."

She writhed under my attention as a nervous giggle escaped her lips. I delivered a playful slap on her ass. "My cock waits for you."

"I thought I wasn't your slave." She playfully slapped me back.

Oh, I loved feisty women.

"And you'd leave my cock to wither?" My voice was small and pathetic. It was a fine bit of play-acting.

She nearly choked, "Oh, there is NO danger of your cock withering." She laughed as her hand slowly moved down my body. "It's been stabbing at me all night." Her fingers twirled around my muscles, teasing my stomach as my cock leaped for her.

I bit down a bit harder on her breast as I spoke through gritted teeth. "Free it and give me some peace, woman!" I lapped at the bitten nipple and slid my hand to her pussy, which I found dripping. I easily slid her moistened panties from her wet lips and danced my fingers around the folds of her sensitive flesh.

"Perhaps a prelude will encourage you," I growled with a voice roughened by sexual need as I dove a finger into her wet center.

Another gasp heated my ear, but her fingers remained painfully slow. "Perhaps I should leave my dark lord's cock where it is since he growls and bites!" she chided, her voice a siren's song.

"For God's sake take it out before I cum in my pants," I growled as I rolled on top of her and stabbed my clothed cock into her.

She licked her lips as she stared at my masked face and deliberately parted her legs for me. Instead of touching me, she wrapped her hands around my back and slid them down my pants to my buttocks and pressed me against her as she ground her pussy into my painful cock. I let her rock herself on me until I felt my balls clench. I was seriously about to cum with just her dry fucking.

"Oh no you don't" I hissed, positioning myself at her center, I grabbed her hands and pinned them to either side of her head, "Leave your hands there," I ordered. "If they won't obey!" I scowled teasing. "There will be torture." I winked.

"Oh, for whom I wonder?" Her lips curled into a beautiful smirk.

I rose to kneel before her, my jaw clenched, my eyes intense. "Since my goddess won't release the monster then I will… and she may regret it." In one quick motion, I lifted her hips and slid her pink silk panties off her body.

Before me was the most beautiful pussy I'd ever beheld. The hair was neatly trimmed around soft lips and a glorious rose-red inner labia protruded with excitement. I leaned in and kissed her pussy, grazing my lips over her glistening folds to the apex where her clit nestled. I just gave her enough to ache for me as badly as I wanted her. I then unsnapped my pants and wiggled my cock free as the air finally soothed my engorged penis. My purple mushroom head was already dribbling pre-cum. Her eyes widened when she saw me finally revealed. I wasn't too large, but I had a thick cock. When fully erect, it was quite a sight.

On a whim one weekend, when I was with a friend at their lake house, he and I and the girls we were dating at the time went into town. It was in rural Wyoming, and the town had a small grocery store, a bar, a tattoo parlor, and an arts and crafts store. We went to the bar and got totally fucking blasted on some private moonshine and went to get tattoos.

I decided I needed an adornment to my cock, so I got a tribal cross tattooed right below my waistline. I also got an arrow on my hand between my first finger and my thumb. The arrow reminded me to always move forward toward my goal, and the one above my cock, well, it was fucking sexy. As soon as I stepped out of my pants, Rey saw the tattoo with the end of the cross pointing straight at my jutting rod. Her mouth opened wide as her face gracefully morphed into an enormous smile.

"You would have a tat right above your cock," she teased, lifting her hand to brush her fingers over the tattoo.

"Ah ah, I told you not to move," I scolded her and gave her a soft slap on the side of her thigh.

"No, I don't play that way." Her smile widened as her hand snaked around my neck, and she lifted her head to kiss me.

Her kiss was so delicious, sweet, and passionate. Her other hand swirled around my tattoo, unintentionally touching my cock and sending me into a frenzy.

"I want to fuck you!" I growled in her ear.

"I want to fuck you too," she growled back.

We both laughed as she finally slid her soft hands over my cock, smoothing the viscous liquid from the tip around the shaft. She moved my foreskin up and down over the bulbous head, sending rockets of pleasure through my body. Feeling frantic, I turned my body around to face the end of the bed and kicked my leg over her face as I planted my face into her amazing pussy. I lapped up the juices that had gathered there, using my tongue to swirl her into an orgasm.

With my cock in her face, I felt her warm mouth kiss the tip, and lap at the still oozing slit. I responded by sucking her clit and sliding my tongue up and down it until she shivered and bucked under me. She was nearing orgasm, so I pushed my tongue into her vagina, reaching as far as I could go. She responded by swallowing my cock into her mouth. We rutted and bucked until we were both almost ready to release. I stopped giving her cunnilingus long enough to pull my penis out of her mouth, turn around, and roll her into my arms.

"I don't want to cum in your mouth." I was being honest. "I want to enjoy you as long as I can." I kissed her cheek, the taste of her still on my lips.

Her legs wrapped around me as she angled her pussy onto the tip of my penis. "I'm enjoying this too." Her voice was hazy and laced with lust as she placed her hot wet pussy over my cock head.

All I had to do was push my way in. For a moment, my thickness was an obstacle, but she slipped her fingers down to her lips to open them for me, and I slid in slowly. She moaned at my intrusion. Her body hugged me tightly, and I could truly say her pussy was everything I'd hoped it would be.

"Oh my God, your goddess vagina is heaven," I breathed into her ear as I began to pump in and out of her.

"Mmmm," was all she was able to utter, her face contorted in ecstasy.

The orgasm she almost had in my mouth came easily on my cock as she shuttered and spasmed around me. With her release came frenzied fucking. Suddenly, I was possessed. I pulled her legs in closer and dug myself as deep into her as I could go. She winced a tiny bit as I must have hit the back of her vagina, but I kissed her through the discomfort. My mouth claiming hers, my body enveloping her body as I rutted into her, feral and unbridled.

I don't know what possessed me; perhaps it was the masks, the games, her beauty. I had no real idea, but I slammed in and out until my balls tightened beneath me, "I'm going to cum in you!" I rasped as I shot a thick load and ejaculated semen deep inside of her.

"Um," she called out as another orgasm gripped her. "Can you pull..." she breathed, trying to find balance within her thrall. "Out?" she sighed as I pumped the last of my semen into her.

I stayed in her, both of us panting and hot. After the heat of the moment had passed, I instantly was hit with a wave of regret, finally comprehending what she'd just asked.

"I'm sorry," I said as I slid my semi-hard cock out of her. "I didn't mean to lose control like that." I hadn't even asked her about birth control, nor had I given her time to tell me what to do when I came.

"It's okay." She smiled, her cheeks flushed and heated. "I knew what I was getting into. It's fine. We're fine." She kissed my lips sweetly.

She'd given me such a gift, forgiveness, and owned her responsibility as well. "If there's anything ... any problem... um." I was unsure of what to say.

If she got pregnant, I didn't know what I'd do. I intended on remaining anonymous. I'd fucked up.

"Whatever happens I'll take care of it. I'm here because I want to be here. It's okay." She kissed me again and was so loving and sweet. "It was amazing. Thank you... I... you're right. I'll remember this for the rest of my life."

We made love twice more that night, and I made sure to pull out of her before I came. We drank more champagne, finished the strawberries, and simply enjoyed each other's company. We also role-played a little more, the captive goddess and her dark-winged hero. By the time exhaustion gripped me, I was feeling warm and amorous. In fact, when she curled her naked body into mine and sleep dragged us away from each other, I was ready to tell her who I was. I wanted to explore what we had just discovered. I was actually excited about seeing where dating her might lead; however, when I woke up in the morning, I was cold, and everything felt empty.

In her place was a note on plain white linen paper provided by the mansion.

"To my Dark Prince. Thank you for the night of my life. I'll never forget you and perhaps may never find your equal. I'm sure you know how special and unique you are. Please know too that I loved you deeply for as long as I was able to have you. Last night you had all of me, which I willingly gave and would gladly give again if our paths should ever cross. May your life be filled with magic and may all your dreams come true. Love, your Captive Goddess."

The note stabbed my heart. She was gone.

Chapter 8

One Year Later

Reyna

Arianna was the most beautiful perfect baby in the world. I couldn't believe she was really mine. Even though I'd given birth to her three months ago, the reality of it was still pretty magical. She was so peaceful when she slept and was the picture of innocence. I marveled at her tiny body, perfect little fingers, and their itsy bitsy fingernails. Her little baby toes were cute enough to eat. I loved this child more than any being on earth.

It was Halloween again, the anniversary of the night I conceived Arianna with the dark mystery angel. I could hear people in the streets shouting and partying. I lived in an apartment in Hollywood, so we didn't get any trick-or-treaters, but there were a lot of Millennials on parade dressed up and having a good time, just like I had last year. I knew what I was getting into that night. I made a conscious choice to be there with him, knowing full well I'd never know his identity. We were so passionate, and so in the moment, I didn't even think or care about birth control. I let him cum in me, and I enjoyed it. I hadn't planned on being a single mother, but when the doctor told me I was pregnant, that was what I became. I wouldn't have had it any other way.

As soon as I saw her little heartbeat, I wanted her, waited for her, and celebrated the day she was born. The love I bore for my little child was unparalleled. I only wished I could thank the masked stranger for his incredible gift. I was feeling nostalgic because Halloween made me remember that perfect night with the perfect stranger. The reality was hitting hard, though, and I had to look for a job again soon. I had a great nanny, an elderly neighbor who had offered to watch Arianna while I worked.

She was ideal for us, kindly, caring, and not too expensive. All I had to do now was find a job and prepare to leave my little kiddo for the first time since her birth. I loved breastfeeding her and co-sleeping in our bed, but it was time for me to make us some money. I still lived with Charlynn and Melody who were as in love with little Arianna as I was. I was doing okay financially; however, my savings wouldn't last forever.

Even though I'd let a stranger impregnate me, it was one of the most exciting things I'd ever done. I still tingled the next morning after making love to him all night. I was sore all over from our exertion but also loved feeling his body still lingering in mine. I loved having his scent on my body. I didn't know then, but his seed was already creating Arianna when I walked away from him that morning.

I left him a note saying goodbye because I knew he only wanted a one-night stand. I couldn't bear to have him kick me out, so I left before he woke up. I thought I would regret that night, but I never have. It was a fun evening, which left me a mother, the best job I've ever had.

Arianna's peaceful and calm nature inspired me to write day and night with her sleeping peacefully in my lap. I even wrote when I was pregnant with her. I found time to write with her sleeping in my lap or nursing at my breast. I discovered voice text on my iPhone, and my world changed completely. All I had to do was talk into my phone and write the bones of the script.

Arianna and I were going to be okay. I just knew we would. It was the strength and power of motherhood that drove me toward success. My life changed when I started feeling sick around Thanksgiving. I realized then I hadn't had my period; I wasn't worried because it was due Thanksgiving week, but I felt off. Somehow, I knew the mysterious stranger and I had conceived a child.

I ignored my queasy nausea, tender breasts, and absent menstruation for a while because Chris kept me so busy with work. After the Halloween party, he asked where I had disappeared to, and I told him I went home. He believed me and said he was only joking about firing me for not going into the room with him. I made sure he understood how illegal it was if it hadn't been a joke.

For some reason, after the party, Chris made me work twice as hard as I had before. When I wasn't running around like a chicken with my head cut off, I was trying to avoid his blatant advances. He must have gotten really pissed when I disappeared on Halloween because he pursued me relentlessly.

"Reyna!" he yelled from his office. "Come in here."

I knew by his bark I had to move fast. So, I rushed into his office with my notepad in hand.

"Yes," I said smiling, keeping my attitude light even though all I wanted to do was puke.

"I want you to tell me if you like these underwear. I just bought a new pair, and I'm not too sure about how they look on me. I was considering throwing out all my old underwear and just buying these, though 'cause… am I wrong? Or do they make my cock look bigger?" He slid his wool trousers to his knees and showed me his underwear. His semi-hard cock was bulging out of the soft fabric, looking lewd and vile.

I rolled my eyes and tried to play it all off as a nuisance. "Pull your pants up, Chris. I couldn't care less about what kind of underwear you want to buy."

"I'm not asking you to care. I want you to tell me if they make my cock look big. Maybe you should come over here and feel it so you can be a better judge of its size. Perhaps it'll inspire you to give me a handjob." My eyes narrowed to a glare, which made him laugh. "God forbid the puritanical Reyna to get on her knees and pleasure me with her mouth." He continued laughing, pretending it was all a joke. "I'm kidding. By your wide-eyed expression, the briefs are having the desired effect. I'll toss my others and get more of these. Also, Rey, you and I are staying late tonight. I got the dailies from the Madhouse Mayhem. You're taking my notes." I hated staying late with him, but there was little I could say about it. At least it was overtime.

"Fine." I rolled my eyes, turned around, and walked out.

That night he ordered us food from an expensive restaurant which we ate while he talked about starting a private production company in the porn industry. He was a mother fucker on all accounts. Of course, he'd go into an industry that exploited women. I couldn't tell if he was actually speaking the truth, and I really didn't care. When it was getting so late I could barely keep my eyes open, he started the movie. We were there until two in the morning. He offered to take me home, but I had my car, so I declined.

"Okay. Well, before you go, I just want you to do one more thing." His face was bloated, red, and lecherous as he dove in for a kiss he literally smashed against my lips.

At the same time, he shoved his hand down my shirt and started groping my breast. I was so shocked and terrified. I started coughing. I was already nauseous 'cause I was pregnant so, when he didn't take his horrible mouth off of mine, I reared my head back and threw up on him. It wasn't a little throw up either; it was a bucket load. Fucking prick, it served him right. He was furious but couldn't say anything because he knew what he was doing. Thank God I did puke, who knows what else would have happened.

"How dare you! You monster." I managed to say after my head stopped spinning. "You're going to have to clean this up, you asshole. I'm going home." With that, I walked out.

I think he was so stunned he didn't even follow me, which was a relief. We never discussed the incident, and it never happened again. We just pretended like nothing happened until my pregnancy started to show.

He walked into the office one morning and went straight to my desk. "You're looking pretty fat these days, Rey. What the hell are you wearing? It looks like a tent." The look of disgust on his face was laughable.

I wasn't really showing that badly. I'd kept my weight down and was eating healthily and exercising, but eventually, little Arianna would show. I knew I was having a girl, and I had decided to name her Arianna after my grandmother who'd died a few years ago. Her name was Arianne, so I thought Arianna was a fitting tribute. I was just about to tell the world I was going to be a single mother, but Chris beat me to the punch.

"You aren't pregnant, are you?" he asked. "Not my little prude? That would be rich. Pretending you're above casual sex and then… boom. I don't see a ring on your finger, so…" His eyes bored right into me.

He wasn't joking this time; he was serious and hateful. It wasn't any of Chris's concern. I was just a temp. I'd actually already told HR I was pregnant. I wanted to keep it a secret from the rest of the office until I was ready to face the music. I started wearing maxi dresses and listened to meditation music at my desk, so people thought I had bought into the newest Hollywood fad; meditation and earthly womanhood was a thing. A thing I actually ended up liking very much.

Human resources were supportive and helped with all the paperwork I needed to initiate my maternity leave. I was a temp, but since I was an in-house temp, I was entitled to some medical insurance and maternity leave. I'd saved up a lot of money, so I was going to be okay financially for a while. I just had to be frugal with my spending.

"That's not very nice to call women fat, Chris," I said, and he slapped my desk.

"We're having lunch in my office. I've got a conference call, and I want you on it to take notes." Fucker! I hated when he made me miss lunch, especially because I was eating for two.

When he said we were having lunch in, it usually meant he'd eat; I'd work and shove food in my mouth after lunch between phone calls. I told myself I just had to last a few more months.

I went in for my working lunch, sitting in the chair across from him when he sat down and just stared at me. "We're not really going to be working," he said plainly.

"Okay?" I eyed him cautiously.

"Look me in the eye and tell me you're not pregnant," he demanded with a dark scowl.

"I can't." I shifted my eyes to my fidgeting hands.

"I thought so." His voice was laced with anger and venom. "Who fucked a baby into you?" How he could be so crass and be the top in the industry truly baffled me.

I lifted my eyes and stared him down. "None of your business."

"You being a whore certainly is my business. What you do on your off time reflects our efforts here," he dared to say.

"Really? And your abysmal reputation for womanizing and sexual misconduct is selling out movie theaters?" Mother fucking hypocrite. "I'm not a whore, and it's disrespectful to assume that just because I choose to be a mother, I'm having sex for money." I glared at him, my tone was accusatory.

"Well, if you'd just fucked me, I would've made sure you never had a baby." This guy was nuts.

"I'd never be with you in a million years, Chris and you know it."

"Apparently, the father of your child feels the same way about you. I haven't seen a man around here paying you any attention, except for the feral assistants who are always sniffing at you. Perhaps you're fraternizing with a co-worker?" His eyes were demonic. "Of course, you know this means you're fired right?"

"Why? Because I'm pregnant? Human resource already knows about the baby. You can't fire me for being pregnant; it's against the law." Oh my God, if I could bring his evil ass down, I would do it in a heartbeat.

"Of course, I could overlook your problem." His eyes shifted back to his usual lecherous expression. "I fucked my wife when she was pregnant with our last child. We did it all the way up until the eighth month."

"Never," is all I said as I stood up to leave.

"If you walk out that door, you don't walk back in again, and your career is over. I'm sure you don't care. You already threw any chance of having a future away when you spread your legs for the rando who knocked you up. Who knew little Miss Priss was getting dick all along." He shook his head in disbelief. "For the record, I'm not firing you because you're pregnant. I'm firing you because you take too many bathroom breaks, and I need you to work hard. I won't be able to spare your maternity leave. I have to train a replacement ASAP. That's what I'm telling HR, and in return, I'll give you a little severance, so you and your unborn bastard aren't on the streets. You're welcome."

I looked at him, tears welling in my eyes, "I hope one day you find a heart, Chris. You desperately need one." I walked out the door, grabbed my coat from my desk, and darted to my car.

I sat in the parking structure and cried for two hours. I didn't really care that I'd lost my job. I was going to leave in a couple of months anyway. I was crying because, as vile as his words were, they hit home. I had let myself down. I allowed myself to get pregnant on a one-night stand by a man I didn't even know and had no way of finding. He could've found me if he wanted because he knew I worked for Chris. He could've hunted me down but didn't, so I was on my own.

I'd suspected Arianna's father was Dragon Kensington, the son of the famous Dirk Kensington. He was the lead in the Dark One movie and was currently filming the sequel. I watched the Dark One several times, and he did have a familiar air about him, but no tattoo on his hand. He may have gotten it after shooting the first movie, who knew. I watched the film over and over again because he reminded me of my dark prince and our incredible night together. If he was Arianna's father, I vowed he'd never know. I'd carry my secret to the grave. He clearly didn't want me, and so I was going to manage on my own. I had a village and an amazing child… I didn't need anything else. This was what I told myself every day. I said it to myself so often, I almost believed it.

I had Jen from HR let me into the office early the next morning, so I could pack up my things. I told her every single word that Chris had said. While I was a temp, and he had every right to fire me, they did have on record some of the things he had done. She told me they were criminal. All I had to do was press charges. She couldn't because they had cameras in the building, but not in his office, per his orders. Without her to testify, it would only be hearsay. Jen was the human resources manager for Chris' company; she couldn't demand that I press charges against Chris, but her pained expression begged that I would.

I was just so overwhelmed with everything that mounting an ugly lawsuit against Chris just seemed wrong. I was happy to be free, and that's all I cared about. Jen gave me a good maternity package, and I was happy. They made sure I was able to stay with the baby for a little while without having to look for work.

Everything was in place; all I needed was a job. I remained friends with Jen after I left Chris' company. So she had requested that I call her when I started looking for work, and she told me about an opening at an incredible independent production house.

Jen explained the job was being an assistant for a man who had a reputation of being devastatingly handsome but could be a hard ass. He'd had his fair share of women but was an exceptionally ethical guy. While I was nervous about entering another assistant job with another controlling man, I trusted Jen, who assured me if I got the job, things would be different.

Chapter 9

Sinclair

I was so tired of interviewing people. Most of the candidates I saw were well-qualified. Any one of them could've filled the executive assistant role just fine. In fact, many of the people I'd interviewed were career assistants. Some were even more efficient than I was. However, despite the quality of the people who interviewed for my assistant position, I was having a hard time finding the right one.

My last assistant was good, gorgeous, and had just booked a reoccurring role on a television series. She deserved it, and I was happy to see her move on to do something she loved and was better suited for. I was happy the job was a launching pad for a person's career. Some wanted to be assistants for life; those weren't the kind of people I wanted working for me. I wanted hungry go-getters who would happily work their asses off to launch their careers. I grew bored with people relatively quickly, and knowing I'd be saddled with someone forever was daunting. I didn't do commitment... at all. Not even at work.

Our company was small and cutting edge. I needed someone cool who would fit our image. I was also a hard nut to crack. I demanded perfection, but also creativity and fun. While I could settle for any of the twenty people I'd already seen, none had that winning combination. This was why I dreaded my last interview of the day.

I wasn't paying attention when the receptionist brought her into my office. I'd busied myself reading the second draft of a movie we'd likely pass on, doing everything in my power to avoid sitting through one more interview. I was seriously considering just having my brother Sage come in and choose the person for me. I was struggling that hard with it.

"Your three o'clock is here," the sweet receptionist said as she opened the door and let the young woman into my office.

I would have hired the receptionist if she hadn't specifically asked me not to interview her for the job. She wanted something low key as she was in her last year of college and was doing an intense independent study. She didn't even like production… that was something I could hardly imagine.

"I can't handle you and independent study," she told me. "I'd explode. Besides, I want to be in finance. Creatives give me the heebeejeebees."

I probably should've been offended, but I wasn't. I knew what she meant. There were days where I didn't even want to handle me or the creatives around the office. When I did finally look up from the script I was reading, the first thing I saw was her beautifully toned legs. My eyes drifted up the rest of her body from her mid-calf length gray wool pencil skirt to her tailored suit jacket. She was a complete and total knockout. Her eyes were a deep dark chocolate color, and her full sensuous lips screamed kiss me. Immediately, flashes of the beautiful masked goddess I had on Halloween night flitted through my mind.

Her beauty was unmistakable. There was no way on earth I wouldn't recognize her, even without the mask. I'm glad she didn't take it off that night, I probably would've been a total beast if she had. She'd left an indelible mark; she'd branded my soul. I knew she worked for Christopher Regent, and yet, I didn't pursue her. She'd left me a note and disappeared. I didn't want to chase her because I was worried reality wouldn't be as good as our fantasy. Also, she certainly didn't need another producer trying to bed her.

It had been exactly a year and a day since that Halloween night, and instead of forgetting her, I still obsessed over her. I Googled Christopher's company searching for her, but nothing turned up. There were a few pictures on the internet I thought might be her; however, they were fuzzy and taken from far away. I often thought of just calling him as we were supposed to discuss some of my projects. Given how Halloween night unfolded, I figured his offer was no longer on the table so, I never called. After spending the night having sex with his assistant, I didn't want to have anything to do with him. I was pretty sure his offer had soured since he saw me snatch her away.

The woman standing before me had the same elegance and grace as my masked lover. I wasn't exactly sure it was her, but I hoped. I'd know if she had the same sharp tongue and quick wit.

"Come on in and have a seat," I said standing with my hand outstretched to the chair in front of me.

"Thank you." She sat down across from me, her eyes deep pools of chocolate brown.

My heart raced. I tried swallowing the parched remnants of my suddenly dry mouth. Fuck, she seemed so much like her… and was gorgeous, simply exquisite. I looked down at the resume before me for the first time.

"Alicia Reyna Sandoval." Her name seemed long and regal. "Tell me a little about yourself." I smiled and straightened up in my chair.

I hadn't even read her resume. I was so disenchanted with the hiring process I hadn't bothered to look. However, when she began to speak, every nerve in my body froze.

"Well, as far as employment goes, my last job was as Christopher Regent's assistant." A shock of electricity jarred me as

I recognized her soft sultry voice.

She smiled innocently, seductively. She wasn't trying to be alluring, but she was that tempting. Alicia… Reyna… Rey… the goddess' nickname was Rey.

"Yes, I see that; however, you have a gap of a few months?" It was an asshole question for an interviewer to ask, but I wanted to know. Did he fire her? Had he made good on his promise? The timeline didn't match up… but something seemed off. She worked until March, and now it was almost the end of October.

"I took some time off to focus on personal stuff. I'm ready to throw myself back into the work world again. Jenna McIntyre, the head of Human Resources at Regent Pictures, suggested this job because you are looking for someone well-rounded and invested in the indie film world… so, I'm your girl." Her smile brightened, and my balls clenched.

"Do you go by Alicia?" I asked, almost panting.

"Um…" she seemed a bit thrown off by my question. "I usually go by Reyna, my middle name. My mom is Alicia, and it got a little weird at home… so… I usually go by my middle name. Everyone just calls me Rey." Her gaze drifted down to the tattoo on my hand, and her eyes widened as her breathing became shallow. "Sinclair… Sin?" she whispered.

I knew then and there it was her. My masked goddess, my muse. My body was so tense and sexually charged. I had to just do it… go there and get it out. I couldn't sit on this.

"Did he fire you because of that night at the Halloween party? As he threatened he would?" I knew I was taking a risk by asking, but I had to know if it was her.

She swallowed hard. Her eyes met mine. For a long time, she just stared at me and didn't say anything. "I'm sorry. I shouldn't have asked."

"No." I think she was too shocked to say anymore.

I tried not to pounce, but it was her! "I wanted to find you."

"I um… I thought you didn't." Her lower lip quivered, and the color drained from her face.

"You're probably overqualified for the job." I laughed, trying to ease the tension in the room. "I'd hire you in a heartbeat, but…"

She took a deep breath. "Do you want me to go?" Her eyes glossed over, and she looked like she might cry.

"No, no… God no. It's just well…" Words… why were words abandoning me? "Do you want to go?" I had to get my game on, but I was struggling, she had such a crazy effect on me.

"No. I don't." She smiled a small, uncomfortable smile.

"Do you think we can do this? Work together?" While we were veering back to normal, it was hard for me to stifle the urge to lunge across my desk, grab her, and fuck her on the floor.

"I think so, maybe. We can try." She swallowed hard and nearly choked. "I can't believe it's you," she whispered.

I stood up and walked over to her. "I can't believe it either, but I'm glad it is." I extended my hand to her, and she took it as I lifted her out of the chair. "You have the job, my goddess. Would you like me to show you around?" Ah… there I was, back in control.

"I'd love that." The glow returned to her face, and I

wrapped my arm around her waist as I pulled her into me, grateful I didn't have a window on the door to my office.

"I'm going to have a hard time resisting you," I whispered in her ear. "But I will… I'll follow your lead. You call the shots. I'm the boss, but our life outside of this office will be governed by what you want. If you want to continue to explore what we started, I'm up for it. If you want to just work for me… I'll adjust." I released her and gave her a sincere smile.

"I think I'd just like a glass of water…" She looked like a deer caught in headlights and was white as a sheet when she suddenly swooned into my arms. I opened the door and called for the receptionist to get us some water, and then lifted Reyna onto the couch.

"What did you do to her, Sinclair?" The receptionist asked in an accusing manner.

"Jitters, I guess." I lied.

The receptionist fanned her face, and Ken from Molly McGrath's office next door brought a wet paper towel from the kitchen for her forehead. I was really worried for a moment because she wasn't coming around.

"Great, you got to stop barking at people, Sinclair," the receptionist scolded.

"I wasn't barking; I didn't yell this time."

She gave me a disbelieving look. Everyone was just standing around, staring. After about five minutes, Reyna finally came to. I put the water on her lips. She drank it and the color, thankfully, returned to her face. The crisis was over. Everyone, the receptionist, my temporary assistant, Christina, and Ken just lingered.

"Okay, it looks like she's okay," I said as I ushered everyone out. "I can take it from here."

"All right then," I hear Ken remark in a disparaging tone. "I hope you hire that one, she's a complete knockout."

"Apparently." I made a joke no one got. I focused my attention back to Reyna. "Are you okay?" I asked as I swiped a wet strand of hair from her face.

Her face was damp and her skin, clammy.

"I'm okay… thank you," she whispered.

Her voice was distant like she'd drifted away and was lost… alone.

"Are you sure? You just passed out. You sure you feel alright?" I'd never seen anyone pass out before. I had no idea what caused such a phenomenon, but I assumed it was stress.

"No… I… feel better now. I think… just, it's you… maybe the shock of it… I'm sorry. I'll go." Her face crumbled.

She looked so broken and tiny. I wanted to scoop her into my arms and love her for the rest of my life. It was a totally ridiculous thought. I was obsessed, but as soon as the obsession wore off, I'm sure my love would too. But I still wanted to try. There was some unseen force driving me… and it was driving me nuts.

"I still want to hire you, despite this little hiccup," I said, offering her another sip of water.

"Really?" she questioned.

"Of course." I resisted the urge to kiss her pale lips.

"Thank you, Mr. Harris." Her voice was small and tenuous.

66

"Woah… Woah. Call me Sinclair. I'm not a Mr. Harris… no, no. Now, I'm very direct. I don't bullshit or mince words. I know you've already suffered a lot with Christopher. I promise I'll never take advantage of you. We don't have to revisit that night or even speak of it if you don't want to. I know how uncomfortable this situation might be."

She seemed to shrink when I mentioned Christopher's name. "It's okay. I want to be here. I just… I… um… I don't want to… oh God." She was struggling so hard.

"Just say it, Rey, it's okay… no judgment." The poor thing was quaking with nerves.

She wasn't the confident woman I'd bedded on Halloween… something was very different about her. Was it possible she wasn't the snarky, sexy girl I'd met? Maybe it was all an act that night or perhaps the mask gave her confidence. Maybe it was doubt, who knew? I decided I didn't care. The mere thought of seeing her every day was enough to get a triumphant rise out of my cock. Keeping it away from her day in and day out was going to be a challenge, so I fully understood her doubt about what we were getting ourselves into.

"Well, you're fully qualified for the position," I was too eager to say.

"But… um… we? Are you sure? We don't ever have to… oh God. It was just a one-night thing, I know. I understand." She was so nervous; it made me worry about her.

"It's okay. I'm happy to hire you. As for the rest, let's just see what plays out." I gave her a reassuring smile.

"Okay." Her face softened, and she seemed relieved.

"Can you start work tomorrow?" I wanted to her start that

minute, but I knew that wasn't a reasonable thing to ask.

"I can," she answered softly.

I helped her get her things, called HR to let them know I'd hired my new assistant, and watched her walk out of my office. At the four o'clock meeting I announced I'd hired the woman who passed out in my office, everyone was shocked.

Chapter 10

Reyna

Of all the men in the world, I interview with him! It had to be him. I had no idea how I was going to pull this off, and I almost called Sinclair and turned down the job. Instead, I decided to just take it one day at a time. I was still so desperately attracted to him, even more now that he wasn't wearing the mask. He had those amazing green eyes and sandy blond hair and a perfectly chiseled face. He looked like a GQ model and oh so... sexy. I didn't know what I was going to do. I was such a mess.

I could see his face in Arianna's; she had his beautiful eyes. I couldn't tell him, though. I didn't want to keep this secret, but I had to. I hoped there was going to be the right time and place to tell him one day, but for now, I was going to focus on work and not letting Sinclair Harris get under my skin. Denial was the best policy... well, it wasn't, but denial was what I was going with.

When I got home to see Arianna's little face, all my worries melted.

"How was she today, Mrs. Effleman?" I asked as I scooped little Ari into my arms.

"The sweetest little angel baby ever," she commented.

"It looks like I got the job. It might be a lot of long hours. Are you okay with that?" I didn't want to lose such a great babysitter. I also knew that with the job and all the complications of my boss being Sinclair, the masked stranger, my life was going to get really crazy.

"Taking care of her is a joy. I'm available whenever you

need me. I'm just down the hall. And, if you ever need a night out or a date, maybe even some overnight fun, I'm here." Her smile was kindly and sweet, but the conversation made me uncomfortable.

"I can get one of my roommates to look after her overnight. I don't want to impose on you. Besides, I won't be having overnight fun." I'm sure I blushed at the mention of "overnight fun."

"You're a beautiful young woman; you shouldn't have to give up your fun or your private life if you have someone to help you with your sweet little babe. I can tell you're a good momma. There will be no judgment from me." Her smile was genuine and endearing.

"I will definitely keep that in mind, and thank you again for today." I kissed little Arianna's head as Mrs. Effleman put her in my arms.

"It's my pleasure. So, when do you start work?" she asked as she stepped into the hall and walked me to my apartment.

"Tomorrow at nine." I gave her a confident smile.

"I'll pick Arianna up at eight," she said.

"Perfect." With that, she waited as I opened my door. "See you tomorrow, little one." She kissed Arianna's head. "See you tomorrow, Reyna."

"Thanks again, Mrs. Effleman." She smiled and went back to her apartment leaving Arianna and me alone for a few minutes before my roommates got home from their jobs.

"Well, kiddo," I said as I closed the door and sat on the couch and offered Arianna my breast which she suckled sweetly. "I'm not sure what Momma's gonna do, but as long as we have each other, I'm sure everything will be just fine."

I told her this but didn't really believe it. I was so nervous my stomach was in knots. What was I getting myself into? When Charlynn got home, I was reading a book with Arianna sleeping in my lap.

"So?" Charlynn whispered. "How'd it go?"

I gave her a half-smile as my stomach catapulted with butterflies. "I got the job."

"I knew you would, and…" She pulled a bottle of chardonnay out of a linen sack. "I brought chilled wine to celebrate. Do you think you can pump and dump for the night? I ordered Taiyoko too. Sushi, Teriyaki, Sashimi… those cute little bento boxes." She was so sweet, and her enthusiasm was infectious.

I loved Charlynn, she was my crunchy granola roommate who was all heart. Last year her luck at the Halloween party was exactly the opposite of mine. She'd actually gotten a text that night from her long-distance thing. They'd been together for two years. He broke up with her over a text proving he was the lame-ass I knew he was. I knew this time of year was particularly painful for her, so the Japanese smorgasbord, which I'm sure would be way too much food for any of us to eat in one sitting, was more for her solace than my celebration.

"Sure, I can pump and dump," I told her. "Little Ari almost sucked me dry just now anyway. I've got tons on ice… we're good."

"Yes!" Charlynn ran to the kitchen, grabbed a wine opener, and popped the cork.

Her red hair shined under the recessed lighting of the

kitchen island, and I thought to myself as she struggled to pull the cork out of the wine bottle, her ex-boyfriend was an idiot. Charlynn was gorgeous, smart, loving… the asshole didn't deserve her.

Our party started. I lay Arianna down in her crib and let Charlynn pour me a fat glass of wine. She had no idea how much I actually needed it. By the time Melody came home, we were halfway through the bottle. Luckily, she brought backup.

"Oh man, you two started already? Guess this means you got the gig eh, Reyna?" Melody was even more casual and laid back than Charlynn.

While Charlynn was a bleeding heart environmentalist with a solid agenda, Melody was our rock star. She was one hundred percent rock and roll diva extraordinaire.

"I got the gig!" I said raising my glass and feeling just a little tipsy.

Luckily Arianna was fast asleep. It hit me; I hadn't even had a drop of alcohol since I found out I was pregnant with her. No wonder the room was floating.

"Right on! Well, I booked a gig for next week that is gonna P.A.Y. like butt loads, so we are gonna be good, girls," she said as she poured herself a huge glass of wine. "What's for eats?"

"Taiyoko!" Charlynn and I both answered.

"Sweet!" Melody planted herself on the couch, and we spent the night eating expensive Japanese food and drinking wine.

It was then I realized no matter what happened between Sinclair and me on this insane journey, I had my girls… all of them.

I walked into the office the next day looking fine. I'd shed my baby weight pretty quickly thanks to hiking, breastfeeding, and everything tasting weird after giving birth. I knew I looked amazing. I only wished I felt amazing too. As I approached my new desk, I saw Sinclair sitting in his office. He seemed stiff and tense. I was immediately nervous, well not just nervous; I was so nauseous I almost threw up.

"Hey, boss." I gave him a small smile.

His face was stern and commanding. He was much more intense without the mask. I preferred him with his mask on. He was playful and sweet when he wore it; now he seemed stern, in charge, and a little intimidating.

"It's nice to see you're here early. Most people barely crawl in on time. That's the film industry for you, late nights, later mornings. Okay. Here's your desk." He waved to my desk as if he were a presenter on a television game show. "And if you want, I have a few minutes to show you around the rest of the office since you passed out the last time you were here."

"I can't believe you hired me. I passed out in my interview. Who does that?" I giggled, discomfort tickling my nerves.

"There was a very significant reason." His face transformed from stern businessman to sultry seducer in a heartbeat.

Behind those smoky green eyes, was the man I made love to on Halloween, my dark prince. My heart raced, and my palms moistened with sweat. The memory of that evening and how we had given ourselves over to pleasure still sizzled my brain. I silently hoped he would be the dark prince again. I wished I was his goddess freed from captivity and he'd ravage me on his leather sectional. I always wondered what captivity he thought he'd liberated me from? I guess he must have been referring to Chris' lurid proposal. Little did he know he only freed me from one captor to deliver me to another; one who stole my heart.

I was now his assistant, playing another role that didn't quite suit me. In my heart, I was a writer with an incredible imagination and now a mother. Assistant with a life-changing secret to hide felt like a thousand-pound weight; heavier than I'd expected it would be.

"I would love a tour," I chirped, probably too enthusiastically, over-compensating to hide my fear.

"It's not a very big office, but it's a little twisted and hard to navigate. This is an art deco building where the stairs go to weird places. The break room is upstairs to the left. That's where most of the staff hang out. Everyone brings their laptops and works there. I think it's because there's free espresso. Sorry to say, you won't spend much time there, though. I need you at my beck and call. Are you a coffee drinker?"

"Not really. I like tea." I made sure to be present and polite, although my insides were melting.

"We have plenty of that too." The tour of the break room seemed to bring awkward to a whole new level.

"Great." I smiled as he grazed his hand over my elbow.

I did everything in my power not to flinch.

"The lobby and the company basketball court are on the mezzanine floor," he said with a straight face, knowing that having a basketball court in the office was probably legendary.

"Are you kidding?" I couldn't help but be impressed.

"Yeah, we're a dedicated bunch, so I tried to throw in a few perks. You'll love Friday at four o'clock cocktails as well. We take shots when we need to brainstorm and throw hoops when we hit a creative wall. As long as we keep cranking out hit movies, I'll keep doing cool stuff for my team." He seemed very proud of his work.

"This is completely different than Regency Pictures. That place is a chrome-plated, minimalist dungeon," I blurted out, without thinking of the horrible incident that brought us together.

"And the Evil Overlord there should probably be indicted for his criminal behavior." He gave me a knowing glance.

"Right, but he'll never... anyway, this place is amazing." I changed the subject, feeling my breath hitch. I hated the memories of my time with Chris, more so now in the presence of the man who rescued me.

"Well... anyway. The rest of the offices are on our floor, and Christina will fill you in on the specifics of the job. I'm sure you'll get the hang of it in no time. And..." he hesitated, "if you have a minute later tonight, maybe you and I can have a conversation?" His voice was a tiny bit shaky as he suggested a private talk. He couldn't have been as nervous as I was? He was this cool alpha indie producer and me ... I was a nervous wreck whose boobs were filling up with milk and making me think of our child who I had hidden away from him at home.

"Sure, I'd love to." My stomach rolled.

"Excellent. I have a meeting in four minutes. I'll touch base with you later." With that, he walked back to his office and shut the door.

I finally took a breath. I searched the office for a place to pump. My breasts were starting to get really painful. If I didn't pump some of my milk soon, I'd be leaking. I didn't want to pump in the bathroom, and yet there didn't seem to be any other place. I wasn't ready to tell HR I had a baby, so I just decided the handicapped stall in the bathroom was going to have to be it. I didn't like the idea of pumping while I was on the toilet, but what else was I to do? I grabbed my bag and went into the bathroom.

As soon as I had expressed all my milk, which took about twenty minutes, I put it in the cooler and returned to my desk. I was ready to get to work.

When I reached my desk, Sinclair was standing there with a frown on his face.

"Did you get lost?" He was being a bit over-lording, but I guess he must've needed something.

"No, I was… um, in the ladies room." I lowered my voice.

"Right, well I want you to join this meeting, please." He was all work. "And let me know when you plan to be away from your desk."

Gone was the sexy masked stranger who I'd only glimpsed a few times throughout the day. The real Sinclair was very intense and somewhat scary.

"You bet," I said, chipper and enthused, trying to lighten his mood as I grabbed my notepad and walked behind him into the office.

Chapter 11

Sinclair

Having her in the office was making me insane. I realized that when I barked at her for not being at her desk. There was no reason for me to go off on her as I did. I was just jealous and territorial. She was thorough and attentive during the meeting and submitted notes about a half-hour after it was done. She was used to hard work, I could tell. By the end of the day, my mood was lighter, and I was feeling more comfortable around my beautiful new assistant who I just wanted to fuck.

Despite being efficient, socially exceptional, and a joy to look at, she did go to the bathroom a lot. She must have had a nervous bladder of some sort. Also, Ken, Molly McGrath's assistant in development was flirting with reckless abandon. I wanted to strangle him and cut off his cock. I didn't like men circling around things that were mine. And yet, she wasn't mine at all. The dashing young man had just as much a right to her as I had. This enraged me. I needed to establish the upper hand. I knew nothing about her other than she was a little shy in bed, sexually responsive… and liked to play. Outside of that, she was just a woman I fucked while wearing a mask, but I wanted her to be so much more.

"See you tomorrow, Rey," Ken, the asshole encroacher, said as he slung his backpack over his shoulder.

"See ya." She smiled and gave a little wave.

Oh, if only murder was legal.

"How was your first day?" I asked as people said their goodbyes and filed out of the office. I leaned casually against her cube and stared at her delicious chocolate brown eyes, remembering the way they looked when I entered her for the first time. I was also trying to abate my jealousy, which was tipping towards unbridled rage.

"It was good. Everyone is really nice and fun. I like it here." Her smile lit up her face, and yet, it didn't seem completely genuine.

"I'm glad you're fitting in. I have a very efficient call log here… so detailed. Nice work. The basic administration is just part of what you'll be doing. I'll have you into more meetings soon, and I'd love to hear your thoughts about our projects, perhaps bounce ideas off of you." I was probably being too nice, too overly enthusiastic and eager, but I wanted her to like working for me… desperately.

"That's amazing, thanks." Her smile brightened more and finally looked earnest.

"Do you mind stepping into my office for a few minutes? I'd like to have a private conversation with you." I tried not to sound like a school principal calling in a naughty child, but I'd been waiting for this moment all day.

"Sure," she said, being tenuous again.

I walked into my office, sat down, and took a deep breath; she did the same.

"What we're doing here is a little dangerous," I started, getting right to the point.

"I know. I… um…" she fumbled.

"Halloween night was amazing, but it was only supposed to be one night, and then we'd go our separate ways." Her eyes drifted to the floor, and I thought she might cry. "I'm not saying this to hurt you."

"Okay," she straightened up in her chair as her lower lip quivered the way it seemed to when she was really stressed.

"When you left the next morning, I was a little crushed," I said, allowing her to see my more vulnerable side.

"You said it was all just for one night... a fantasy." Her eyes were wide and confused.

"Don't worry. You were perfect. Leaving a note was a sweet touch. However, I didn't think you'd get under my skin, but you have. You working for me adds some complication, but I'd still like to explore what we've started. How do you feel about that?"

"Um, I'd like to explore it too. But... I work for you." Her voice was small and tentative.

"I know, and I'm not really anybody who does long-term relationships. This is why you working for me is dangerous. I'm afraid you might get hurt." Now I was feeling off-center and nervous. Fuck my honesty sometimes.

"I understand." She was pulling away.

"As I said. I don't want to hurt you, but I'm an asshole. You'll discover that soon enough. I'm not a monster like Christopher Regent, but I'm still formidable. If you want to back out now, I'm giving you a license; you can say no. Just because I can't seem to get through a day without thinking about fucking you doesn't mean you have to agree to this." Well, now it was out there.

She bit her lip and stared at me for a beat. I honestly thought she might walk away.

"I think I'm okay with it, just be gentle. I really haven't had that many relationships. I'm not good at getting my heart destroyed. And… just fucking? That's gonna be tough." Her wide eyes were so innocent and earnest.

"I don't plan to destroy you, love. You'll probably tire of me first. I'm not an easy man to reckon with, sadly. I can't deny my attraction to you, and I'm selfish enough to tempt uncharted waters to explore these feelings. And… yeah. Fucking. Why did I say that? I want to do way more than just fuck you. In fact, I really want to kiss you right now," I asked, while not really asking.

"Perhaps it's best we did not explore this in the office," she so reasonably said.

"Right, we shouldn't." Damn her for being so sensible.

"I want to have sex with you again. Is there a chance of that happening someplace else?" What the hell was wrong with me?

She laughed. It felt good to hear her laugh.

"I loved our night together, Sinclair, and I want to make love to you too. It would be amazing, but now that you're real, I think we should take it slow. You were my dark prince before; now you're my boss. Reality can be a little stifling." Her voice quivered, but she was being honest.

"Right. Well, I'm starving… how about I treat you to a sausage." She burst into laughter.

After a moment I got the joke, "I mean… there's a place… a stand downstairs.

Her face shifted into a smirk as she stared at me.

"Ah, forget me… I'm a mess."

"I'd love a sausage." She continued to laugh. "This is gonna be so hard."

"So just fuck me." I flashed her a spectacular grin. "Right, I know. I'm being too primal."

"If only I could." She stood up. "But I have to work in the morning, so I'm just going to eat sausage with you. Not to be confused with eating your sausage." She winked... there she was.

"Okay." I was disappointed, but I understood.

"For tonight." She gave me an encouraging smile.

I helped her put on her coat, and we walked downstairs to the hot dog stand on the corner.

"We can go to Morty's across the street if you want, they've got better food." I didn't want to take my goddess to a hot dog stand; this was ridiculous. Morty's was a nice place. But work people went there, and seeing us together, especially after her first day of work, may look a little suspicious. I was losing my mind.

"Hot dogs are fine," she said as we walked out of the office and down to the little stand in front. "This place actually has like fifty-five-star reviews on Yelp, it's famous," she encouraged as she slid onto one of the dilapidated bar stools surrounding the hot dog shack.

"You sure?" I slid in next to her.

"Positive." She grabbed my hand and gave it a squeeze.

I scooped up a menu, even though I knew what my order would be. I always ordered the same thing, Italian sausage with onions and mayonnaise, disgusting but delicious.

We placed our orders. She had a veggie dog with ketchup, and then we sat there staring at one another.

"So why don't you want to be with me tonight?" I asked, always one to speak my mind.

"If you're not one for commitment then… I don't want to burn you out too soon." She stared at her tofu dog when Artie, the hot dog guy, handed it to her. "This looks yummy." I think she was serious.

"How can tofu be yummy?" I was so bewildered; why didn't she just get a regular hot dog.

"Shut up. I like it." She was so intoxicating.

"I sound like a complete bastard, don't I? About everything. Sorry." I traced my finger along her forearm.

"I get it. You're used to being you. No commitment, real meat hot dogs." She took a bite of her dog, ignoring my touch. "I don't know you. So …" she looked at me again. "Tell me more."

"What would you like to know?" I asked unsure of what to divulge.

"Well, why did you start a production company?" It was an innocent question but felt like she was purposefully avoiding the passion.

I'd only slept with a few women since that Halloween party. Nora, my regular fuck buddy, and I were losing our spark. The sex was just okay, and we were both too busy to make time for "just okay" sex. I also slept with an old flame, but there weren't many sparks left there either. And there she was, my goddess and yet something had changed. She was still sexy as all hell, but distant.

I laughed at her question about my production company. "Seems like you're interviewing me. Okay. I'm really a nerd. Going to the movies was like going to church for me. I always wanted to create magic across seventy feet of a movie screen. It was a dream I made a reality." I shrugged and took a bite of my dog.

"You certainly don't look like a nerd." She cocked her head and took another bite of her hot dog… thing.

"What does a nerd look like exactly?" I was curious to hear what she thought.

"Not like a Calvin Klein model, that's for sure."

"While I appreciate the compliment, I'm no model. And why can't nerds be handsome? Are you nerd-hater?" I tried to loosen her up by teasing.

"I'm not hating. I'm a nerd too. I know exactly that feeling you get when you go into a movie theater. Being like a church perfectly explains the kind of reverence movies can inspire in a person."

"And what about you? What kind of nerd confession do you have for me?"

"I'm an only child. My parents are in Ohio; they're really in love with each other. It's sweet. They had me later in life, so they're pretty old but still look at each other with such an incredible glow in their eyes." She sighed and smiled, fighting off the urge to say more. "They own a farm. Everything they do is about their farm. I didn't end up being a farmer and that sort of disappointed them, but it just isn't in my blood. I didn't like the farm and especially didn't like watching them render the chickens. I became a vegetarian. They weren't too surprised. They were sad when I moved to California but wanted me to follow my dreams. Pretty typical I guess." She shrugged her shoulders.

"I'm pretty sure nothing about you is typical," I said as I scooped her hand into mine and kissed her knuckles. I wanted to kiss every inch of her, but I was showing restraint.

"You and I have a lot in common it seems." She took another bite of her tofu dog and looked at it. "These are really good. I can't believe a roadside hot dog stand has veggie dogs, that's pretty epic."

"It's Hollywood. You're not the only weirdo here," I played.

"I'm not weird." She screwed her face into a knot and crossed her eyes. Her beautiful face looked hilarious.

"I have to confess. I invited you here to the Dog Haus instead of to Morty's across the street because, as per your request, we'll take this slow. If you were to be seen with me at Morty's, you'd be news."

"Well, thank you." She finished her dog. "The veggie dog was amazing... and so is the company." She tentatively squeezed my hand.

"The Dark One Two, Darkness Falls is premiering a week from this Friday. It's going to be a big event, and I'd like to invite you as my date. What do you think?" I silently prayed she'd say yes. No more playing around, I needed her to know I wanted her and not just as a dinner buddy, but as a goddess writhing under me just as she had before.

"Won't people in the office think I'm dating you if we go as a date?" She nervously twirled her fingers.

"If they do, they can find another job." I was deadly serious; nothing was going to keep me from exploring a relationship with her. "We'll play assistant and boss for the premiere, but I want you to stay the night with me after. You won't be working for me then."

"Well then, I guess I need to get a fancy dress." Her face was exquisite when she smiled.

After hot dogs, we went back to the office. I offered to take her home, but she was stubborn and independent and refused to let me.

The next day at work, I had a hard time concentrating on anything other than her. I found myself calling her in several times a day to watch dailies or read script pages for her thoughts.

Most of her suggestions were surprisingly good. She really knew her stuff. I was so tempted to take her out again, but she told me she had to get home. We worked, and she left without me for the second day in a row. Worst, she walked out with Ken, who held the elevator for her, which burned me up. The rest of her first week, she was efficient, creative, and fun; just what I had ordered. She spent a lot of time in the bathroom and seemed to rush off right after we finished our work. It was almost as if she didn't want to spend time with me.

I was probably being paranoid, but I worried she might be doing drugs or had a boyfriend. She was holding something back, and it started to eat at me. It was weird; she didn't have a cocktail on Free For All Friday. When the weekend came, I invited her to a friend's horror movie party, and she said horror films freaked her out and declined.

"You aren't going to like our most famous movie then," I tried to tease and scold at the same time.

"I love it," she countered. "It's because... well... the lead character reminds me of you. And for a minute, I thought you were Dragon Kensington." She actually blushed after admitting that.

"Oh my God, Dragon is a total stoner and a diva-asshole.

He'd chew right through you. Be glad I'm not him." We had a good laugh over that, but still, she refused all of my offers saying she was saving herself for the premiere.

"Well then, it's gonna be one helluva night. I just want to warn you now, don't plan on going home on Saturday." I gave her a seductive wink and let her go on her way.

I wasn't sure what game she was playing, but it was working. I wanted her more than ever, even if she was a drug addict with a boyfriend.

Chapter 12

Reyna

Working for Sinclair was much harder than I thought it would be. The work itself was fun and easy, but he was intense and brooding. Handsome, devastatingly handsome, but always around. He was like a control freak puppy. I wasn't regretting my decision to date him; only he scared me a little. At work, we bantered and flirted, or tried to flirt without being caught. He had insane jealousy for Ken, who I had absolutely no interest in. Seeing Sinclair get all crazy was fun, though.

I kept our relationship professional at work. I didn't go out with him again after our hot dog date even though he asked several times. I wanted the premiere to be special and... I needed to get home to Arianna on time. If I was out every night, I'm sure Mrs. Effleman would have something to say. Little did Sinclair know, but I was making our daughter my priority, even if I was just starting to date her dad.

The day of the big movie premiere and our date arrived. I was excited for both. I'd been so busy at work getting ready for the premiere I was happy to finally see the finished product on the big screen with an audience. I'd seen it in Sinclair's office a hundred times, or at least it seemed like a hundred times, it was probably only four.

I borrowed a dress from Melody who was exactly my size. I didn't really want to spend money on an expensive dress and knew Melody had a ton of cool clothes. She was a consignment store shopper and got amazing deals. I never had as much luck as she did finding things. I always ended up sifting through endless rows of taffeta and lace. She could sort out the one gem amid the sea of poofy prom dresses; I could not.

I had to admit, I looked good.

"Girl you are gonna set that place on fire," Charlynn said as she cradled Arianna in her arms.

I bit my lip. "Are you sure you guys are going to be okay?" I'd never left Arianna overnight before. I felt so delinquent.

"Oh, my God." Melody plopped down beside her. "We are going to be so fine. A hundred percent fine! Ari is the cutest, sweetest baby in the whole world. Be gone all weekend; we can hack it."

"She's right, Rey. We got this," Charlynn added.

"I might come home Saturday even though he wants me to stay," I warned.

"Oh no, please don't. You have a great night, get some... get a lot and don't even worry one bit." Charlynn gave me a seductive smirk.

"Have some for us. I haven't had sex in for-ev-er..." Melody playfully pouted.

"Oh my God... why did I tell you he wanted me to sleep over?" I covered my face with my hands, just wanting it all to go away.

"You're acting like a brat. Be a woman. We know you. You had sex with the amazing mystery guy/baby daddy, and now your boss wants a sleepover. It's okay to explore your sexuality, Rey. You're not in a convent. You can have sex with more than one man in your life," Charlynn chided.

"I've been with more than one man!" I protested. I'd actually only been with two, but they didn't know that yet. I hadn't told them that my boss and the mystery man were one and the same. When I asked for a night out, they both encouraged me to accept his offer to spend the night.

"Have fun and enjoy it. We'll be here lovin' on this sweet baby of yours, just wishing we were you." Melody smiled as she took the sleeping Ari from Charlynn's arms and carried her to the crib.

"Now get out of here before you're late," Charlynn said as she stood up and pretended to shoo me out. "You look hot as hell, go burn up the town you fucking goddess and don't come home until you are spent!" Charlynn literally pushed me out the door. "The three of us are gonna be just fine."

I looked back at her before she shut the door in my face. "I love you," I said through the door.

"Back at ya, now get out of here."

Butterflies roared to life in my stomach, and I thought I was going to be sick. I had insisted on taking an Uber to the theater even though Sinclair offered to pick me up. He almost demanded that he come to get me, but I lived at the opposite end of town, and he had dinner arranged with the filmmakers. There was too much going on, and I finally got him to admit it, so I promised to be on the red carpet at eight o'clock sharp.

I arrived with time to spare. I was standing there when he walked up behind me and slid his hands over my body. Melody had given me a teal gown that hugged my curves. It was made of soft silk, just like the dress I'd worn on Halloween night, but this dress was also adorned with a little rhinestone flourish at the bottom.

"You look good enough to eat," Sinclair breathed in my ear.

I turned around a little startled. "Hello." I smiled as I leaned back into his embrace.

"Are you ready to stop avoiding me now?" he asked, sounding almost menacing.

"Me? Avoiding you? Why would doing my job be an avoidance? Such a strange boss you are." I caressed my hand over his arm.

"Well, you won't be anything tonight but my date." He bit my earlobe and looped his arm around mine. "Ready to face the masses?"

"Not really. Remember, I'm still your assistant until we get to your house."

He gave me a playful glare.

"I mean. Yes… of course, yes."

I wrangled my enormous bag as we made our way into the theater. I'd brought a change of clothes and my cooler. The last thing I wanted to do was leak breast milk onto Melody's beautiful dress. I couldn't wear my heavy-duty, never leak on anything bra… it was absolutely not sexy at all and would look hideous with the dress. I wore something lighter… and less leak proof.

"I see you brought an overnight bag," Sinclair mentioned with a seductive smirk.

"One can never be too prepared," I joked.

"Apparently not. You certainly are welcome to stay for the weekend. It looks like you packed for it."

With that, we walked into the theater. As soon as we stepped into the huge, packed theater, my heart fluttered and then sank. Standing three rows ahead of us was Christopher Regent with Reed Knightly, his head of production.

"We'll walk right past them. We have special seating at the front." He looped his arm around mine and moved me forward.

I hoped Chris wouldn't see us, but he took notice the minute we passed. I didn't dare look at his face, but I could feel the heat of his stare. I think Sinclair sensed it too because he stiffened as we walked down the aisle to our seats.

"I'll make him suffer, don't worry," Sinclair whispered to me under his breath.

As we made our way to the seats, Sinclair spoke to a host of people all clamoring for him as we made our way down the aisle. Most of the people he talked to noted me but didn't say anything. Sinclair was gracious, a perfect showman. I was relieved when we finally were able to slide into our seats in the VIP section.

The film started shortly after we sat down, and it was a tremendous success. The audience responded perfectly to the horror and gore. The hero in the film, the Dark One, was just as handsome, sexy, and heroic as ever. I couldn't help remembering when Sinclair had dressed as the fallen angel and seduced me so completely that night. It made me excited for our evening ahead.

He held my hand through the whole movie. His wayward thumb stroked my skin, and a few times, I saw him adjust himself. He was very excited about the evening ahead, I could tell.

The film was so dark and sexy. In the second installment, Dante and Analisa fight off rogue angels who are trying to abduct all the young women of the world to serve in their coven. Having his father's blessing Dante infiltrates the dark angel lair and with a lot of fighting and blood, frees the captives. I loved the film, but I hoped they'd hire a woman writer for the third installment. The film was good but could use a woman's take. I mentioned it to Sinclair when the credits were rolling, and I was surprised he'd never thought of the idea.

"Wow, a woman writer and director might be an excellent direction to take this. Reyna, you're a genius," he praised, his hand nonchalantly smoothing over my thigh. "Is there anything you aren't good at?" he asked, enamored.

"Oh, there's plenty."

Sinclair was beaming. This was his life's mission, and he was proud of this accomplishment. Most of the people stayed until the last credits rolled up the screen. This might have been because they liked the film, or their name was so far down the credit list they had to wait to see it. Either way, Sinclair was very happy.

"Looks like this film might be a bigger success than the first." His voice had an excited trill. This was really his moment. "And I love your idea of taking in a more feminine direction with the next one… fuck, this feels good!"

"You've worked really hard, you deserve this," I complimented. "The audience loved it," I said when the lights came up.

"You worked hard too." Not sure why he was including

me; it made me laugh. "What?"

"I did, for a whole two weeks. I worked hard." I playfully punched his shoulder. "Just enjoy this; it's all yours."

A throng of people was clamoring to get to Sinclair and congratulate him. It felt like we were going to be in the theater forever. We also had an after-party to attend. Sinclair promised me we'd only stay long enough to make an appearance. After we'd said "hi" and schmoozed with enough people, we'd sneak out.

His plans were for a romantic dinner at his mansion in the Hollywood Hills. He had offered me a choice. A romantic dinner at a nice restaurant or his personal chef, Salvatore, creating something exciting at home for just the two of us. Of course, I choose his house. The farther away we were from people who knew him and might recognize him while we were out, the better.

Sinclair was polite and succinct with all of his admirers, and I was actually impressed at how quickly we were making our way toward the exit when Chris stepped in front of us and stopped us in our tracks.

"What a glowing success, Sinclair. I truly did not think the sequel was going to hold. I'm pleasantly surprised," he said with a note of polite maliciousness.

"I'd say it's even better than the first. Glad you enjoyed it." Sinclair was curt and direct.

"I'm disappointed you never followed through on my offer last year to discuss projects. I think I probably could have gotten a lot better production value for the price, but I'm still open to a meeting. Just give my office a call." Chris handed Sinclair his business card as he eyed me.

He hadn't made eye contact with me until that point as if

he was waiting like a viper in the grass for the perfect moment to strike. My blood stopped pumping, and I felt like I was going to be sick. Fear and loathing… that's all I had flowing in my veins.

Sinclair took the card. "I'll look at our line up and see if anything fits." I was hoping Sinclair was only mentioning this just to be polite. I couldn't fathom working with Chris again. "I'm glad you enjoyed the show. We actually have to get to the party venue and check on everything before the guests arrive. It was good talking to you." Sinclair tried to walk past Chris, but he didn't give way.

"I certainly hope I'm on the guest list." Chris began to seethe.

"Of course, it's at the Chateau Marmot. We'll see you there." Sinclair's tight expression was starting to give way to anger when Chris finally stepped aside to let us pass.

I was so relieved I finally let out a sigh when Christopher reached out and grabbed my arm. His eyes were vicious and cold.

"Oh, and Reyna, you look absolutely fantastic. No one would ever guess you just had a baby. You certainly can't tell by looking at you. I can't believe you got that gorgeous flat stomach of yours back. I thought women's bodies went to hell after having a child. You prove that theory wrong." His voice was an evil hiss.

"Excuse me!" Sinclair was about to snap. "Please take your hand off of my girl… assistant." His eyes were wild and territorial.

"Did you have a girl or a boy?" Chris continued.

I froze in my tracks, terrified, and stared at him. I didn't know what to say. After an uncomfortable beat, I finally was able to form words. "I don't want to discuss it." My voice was a flat monotone.

Sinclair took my hand and pulled me up towards the exit. "I don't know what this is all about Christopher, but Reyna and I need to be going." He moved us away, but it wasn't fast enough.

"What? Did you give it up for adoption or something?" His last remark was cruel and biting.

As Sinclair marched us away, tears welled in my eyes. He pulled me closer and whispered in my ear, "Are you okay?" His voice was laced with worry and concern.

"I'm fine," I responded feeling blindsided and terrorized. "Can we talk about it later?" I asked, even though I didn't know what I'd say when we did bring up the subject again.

I couldn't tell him about Arianna. I wasn't ready to let him know she was his. If I told Sinclair that what Chris had said was true… he might jump to the wrong conclusion. We let ourselves get carried away on Halloween. I told him that night I hadn't been with many men. Now I'd have to say I'd gotten pregnant and had a child with someone else? I have no idea what he'd think of me… and worse, it would be a lie. Dread filled my veins, and my body became as heavy as lead.

Chapter 13

Sinclair

As we made our way out of the theater, I was stunned to silence. My mind was scrambled with thoughts. I couldn't even put them together properly. She had a newborn baby from the sound of it. Whose was it? When did she have it? It had to have been within the year. Was it Christopher Regent's child? I couldn't let the night pass without facing this, so when we got into the limo, I put up the privacy screen and confronted her.

"I know you told Christopher Regent you didn't want to talk about it, but I feel like I should know the truth." I was somber and disoriented.

"I know," was all she said as she began to cry.

"So, you do have a baby?" Even saying the words increased the weight of my shock.

"I do," she whispered.

"Why didn't you tell me?" I was prying, but this was a woman I was trying to get to know better.

I fully intended on bedding her. Yet as I stared at her gorgeous face flushed red with shame, I realized I knew absolutely nothing about her. She'd withheld the truth from me, and I wasn't sure why. I guessed having another man's baby wasn't something she wanted to share. I understood. In my opinion, though, trust was important in a relationship, and the trust between us was tenuous at best.

"I didn't know how to tell you," she confessed as her eyes drifted down to her lap.

"Sinclair, I have a baby at home..." I teased, trying to get her to relax a little.

The evening wasn't feeling much like a date anymore. I'd waited so long for this. Well, it was a little over a week... and a year. It felt like an eternity. I was fully intending on fucking Reyna all night long, and here I was feeling morose and guilty for some weird reason. Maybe it was because she was paralyzed with fear.

"Sinclair, I have a baby," she said in a strange robotic fashion.

"Where's the father? Are you with him?" What a stupid question, I was so off-center.

"No..." Her lip started trembling as she continued to cry.

"Okay. It's okay. You don't have to talk about it if you don't want to." I pulled her into me and stroked her knee. "I'm here. We can talk about this if you want or don't it's okay." Even though I should have been angry and jealous, all I wanted to do was offer her love and support.

So, she'd fucked a few guys. I was no less guilty of enjoying carnal pleasure. It's strange she seemed so timid with me on Halloween. I was under the impression she was relatively innocent in bed. Guess I wasn't as good a judge of character as I thought I was.

"I'm not a slut," she blurted out her sobs seizing her. "I don't just... I don't usually..." She was starting to heave and buck, crying harshly.

"Hey, it's okay. We make mistakes." I thought I was being helpful.

"She's not a mistake," she said through her tears.

96

"Of course not. I didn't mean your daughter. Clearly, I'm not helping." I sighed as I swirled my hand on her thigh, hoping I was giving her comfort.

"I'm sorry I didn't tell you," she whimpered so softly, I barely heard her.

My hand on her knee swirled with sensual strokes, sending her the message I still wanted her very much, despite this new revelation. "So, it's a little girl?" I thought talking about her daughter might help.

"Arianna," she cried softly as tears dripped out of her eyes.

"It's a beautiful name. Does the father know?" I know the question was probably indelicate given her state of mind, but she was so broken I couldn't go on without getting us through this.

"No," she whispered.

"Don't you think you should tell him? Perhaps he wants to know he has a baby." It wasn't very romantic, and I should have been happy to have him out of the picture, but suddenly I felt bad for this father who had a child in the world he may never meet.

"I don't think he wants her." She turned her tear-stain face and looked directly at me.

There was something in the look, something that said it all. Of course, she wasn't a slut or a drug addict. She was still that timid, sexy woman who gave herself over to a night of pleasure. One night where she stopped caring and lived the fantasy. One night with me in a mask.

"Have you asked him if he wants her?" I looked at her with that same wide-eyed earnestness.

She took a deep breath and trembled. Her eyes lowered,

97

and she fumbled with her dress as she spoke. "He was the most beautiful man I'd ever met. He was sexy and kind. I thought I was someone else that night, someone magical." Her eyes drifted back up to mine. "We created a miracle. She's so beautiful." She looked like she wanted to say more, but words choked in her as she stared at me and trembled.

"Is she mine?" I felt the electricity spike between us.

She nodded her head and quietly affirmed, "Yes."

My hand continued to caress her, but my mind bottomed out... I was a father.

"I can take care of her. You don't have to do anything, and if you don't want this ...it's fine I can get an Uber home... I can get another job. It's okay, it's okay." The tears were racing down her cheeks again. "I'm sorry."

"Woah... Woah. Reyna. It's okay." I held her tighter. "I'm a little shocked, but I'm not surprised. This doesn't change anything. I mean it changes a lot, but we can handle this. We're grownups." I think I was counseling myself more than I was her.

I was a father. It was almost too much for me to process. For the rest of the ride, we just held one another and didn't say more. I was actually relieved when we drove up to the Chateau Marmot to have the distraction of a party to ease the tension that had built between us.

I took her hand before we got out of the car and looked her in the face. "I still want you, Reyna. I'm not going anywhere. You can stop crying." I wiped the tears from her eyes. "There's no crisis. We didn't use any protection. I came in you, and we tempted fate. Fate brought us a little girl. I'm sure she's just as beautiful as her mother and the rest... well, we'll work out the rest." I meant every word.

We were already in dangerous territory, which just got a little more harrowing. I could do this, and if I couldn't, well, we'd break up, and I'd offer child support.

"You're not angry with me for not telling you?" she said through her sniffles.

"I wish you felt like you could've told me. I guess I'm upset you didn't trust me enough to say something. I understand though; we don't really know each other. I hope you're more honest with me going forward." I smiled as I tucked a tear dampened strand of wayward hair that always was in her face, behind her ear. Even though she'd been crying and was in distress, she was still so beautiful. Her tears only highlighted her humanity and vulnerability.

"I promise, Sinclair, no more secrets," she whispered.

"I may not be comfortable with commitment, and we might not last, but I promise to honor my role as a father. I hope you begin to feel free to talk to me about anything. Despite what happens, I'll always be here." I was stepping way out of my comfort zone, making this promise. It was the right thing to do, and I knew it. I hadn't worked out the logistics, but it was responsible.

"Thank you." Her smile had returned… finally.

"I still want to be with you tonight. Nothing changes my desire to wine and dine you and fuck you silly. Let's not ruin something that might be amazing before it even begins." I stepped out of the car and offered her my hand.

"Okay. I'll trust you." Her deep brown eyes penetrated me as I held her. I wiped the tears from her face one more time before we went in.

She took a compact out of her purse and patted the red spots on her nose and cheeks. "I look a mess," she lamented.

"You don't. You're beautiful, with or without makeup."

She reapplied her lipstick, smacked her lips, and gave me a playful grin. "But I feel better with it," she said as she put her lipstick away.

"We're going to have to work on that." I smacked her beautiful round ass and walked her into the party. "Let's get in and out of here so I can see what your mom bod looks like without clothes..." I whispered in her ear as her eyes went wide.

Oh, tonight was going to be so much fun.

The party was a bit of a blur. I must have still been in shock from discovering I was a father. As I'd promised Reyna, we made an appearance, spoke to key players, and listened to heartfelt words of congratulations. After about an hour, I snuck her out the back door where a driver was waiting for us. We opened a bottle of champagne in the car and started our evening together.

I had several cars; one was a vintage Volkswagen Westfalia. I loved to drive to the beach and camp by the ocean on occasion. Sometimes being near the sound of waves crashing all day and night was just what I needed to get my mind off things. The Westie had a bed that popped out of the roof and the most basic kitchen set up. It was a perfect rebellion against my over-privileged life.

I also had a Land Rover I drove to work, and this car, the town car, was as luxurious as cars got. It had a small bar and snack table inside. Everything was automated, and if I wanted to fuck her on the back seat, they reclined all the way back. This car was actually my father's, but he was never in the country long enough to drive it. As soon as I got Reyna into the car, I pulled her to me and kissed her. I'd been waiting a year and change to kiss that amazing mouth, and I didn't have the patience to wait any longer.

She opened her mouth for me, our tongues tasting one another as if we were starving for each other. Her fingers twisted into my hair and pulled me in. It took all my willpower not to fuck her in the back of my dad's town car. I had a beautiful evening planned for us. We weren't two teens at the prom; I could hold my cock back for a few more hours.

I never brought women home; this was going to be a first for me. I'm not sure why I wanted to be so intimate with her at first, but after what she revealed, I'm glad I took the risk. Usually, I took women to a hotel.

"Thank you again for understanding about Arianna," she said when our lips parted, and the car started winding up the Hollywood hills.

"Thank you for finally telling me I had a daughter." I offered a sincere smile, so she wasn't intimidated. "Are you hungry?"

"I'm starving." She made a goofy face, and I got to see the fun and silly side of her had returned. Thank God.

"Fantastic. Salvatore is one of the best chef's in the world. I'm sure he'll be happy to be cooking for more than just me." That was a bit of a painful confession, but it was true.

My mom and dad hired me a chef, knowing I'd never cook on my own. All three of their sons have a maid, chef, and butler. They were raised with money and couldn't think of their children not having these basic conveniences. My parents choose to live in various places around the world. They made their money in Los Angeles but prefer to live abroad. The house I lived in was their house, but they never came home to it. They gave it to me, sort of.

I redecorated it and managed their affairs, should they ever want to return. They always assured me they didn't. Sage lived in their weekend house in the mountains, which was basically a complex and Shelton had their loft downtown. They also gave me a small bungalow on the beach in Malibu, which was my secret man lair.

"Wow Fallen Angel films must be doing amazingly well if you can afford your own chef," she said, impressed.

"I have a little confession to make of my own."

She took a deep breath as she waited for me to reveal my secret.

"My mom and dad are billionaires a few times over. We've always had money. My grandfather had an oil company. Currently, my dad is running a real estate development business from an office in London, and my mom is an online self-help guru. They have more money than they know what to do with. My brothers and I just had to pick what we wanted to do with our lives, and my parents funded it. I didn't have to be much of a success, just happy. One of my brothers is in a rock band, and the other is a nasty lawyer who rips people off. I love films, and I got to see my dream come true. Now, I'm pretty much independent, but they do insist on my paying for my chef because they know I probably won't ever attempt to cook. If I did, I'd burn their beautiful house down… and speaking of the beautiful house… we're here."

The car pulled up to the drive, and the driver exited to open Reyna's door.

Her mouth opened wide. "Holy guacamole," she exclaimed with awe.

I laughed, "Did you just say that?"

"I think so," she laughed too.

I adored her.

Chapter 14

Reyna

His house was incredible. It was the kind of place you drove by and fantasized about who lived there. It was massive. I couldn't imagine living there by myself; I'd be so scared and lonely. I thought of the tiny apartment I shared with the girls in Hollywood. I'd switched rooms with Melody, who had the master bedroom when I was pregnant. I wanted the ensuite bathroom for my nightly pee, and it had a small changing area I made into a nursery with a crib, dresser, and changing table. It was perfect for Arianna and me.

Melody used my old room to record her music and actually lived in our dining room. Our house was built in the 1920s and had a dining area offset from the living room and kitchen. We just put doors on it, and she had an incredible bedroom. I only ended up paying a little more for the master bedroom, and Melody continued to pay her share, and Charlynn was happy her rent decreased. It was a win for everyone.

We were cozy in our crazy little apartment overlooking the hills. He, however, lived in this mansion mostly by himself. The place was overwhelming. I knew my mouth was hanging open, but who lived as he did? It was insane.

"It's just you and the chef living here?" I asked, probably sounding dumb.

"There are a housekeeper and butler too," he mumbled.

"All for little ol' you?" I know I was being an asshole, but it was too much... he was like a little rich boy bouncing around his massive estate all alone. It was sort of classic.

"I have friends over." He smiled. "But yes, I'm a little high maintenance."

"A little?" I teased.

We walked to the front of the house, and he opened the door. The house was even more gorgeous inside. Deep mahogany wood, black and white checkered tiles, fixtures, and details preserved to perfection. This house was as old as our apartment but lacked the chipping paint and cracked tiles. It was pristine and perfectly kept.

"It's like a museum," I blurted out in wonder.

"Yeah… it's in some historical catalog somewhere. Do you want a glass of wine?" He was diverting my attention from the extravagance of his wealth, and I welcomed it.

"I'd love a glass," I said as he ushered me inside.

"We have everything, what would you like?" I couldn't imagine a man who had every kind of wine on hand. I guess my imagination wasn't very good.

"A glass of chardonnay would be nice." I tried not to sound awestruck.

This night was nothing like I thought it would be. His house was massive and crazy grandiose, and I just felt lost in it, and I couldn't believe I told him about Arianna. He handled it so much better than I expected he would. I was happy about that. Ariana didn't deserve to be hidden. I wasn't ashamed of her, and neither should he be. No matter what happened between us, parenthood was forever, and I'm glad he understood. The more I learned about Sinclair, the more I began to like him.

"I redesigned most of this myself," he boasted as he walked me past the foyer to the living room with a picture window and an incredible view of the Hollywood hills. "I'd love to show you all I've done to the place, but I don't want to scare you off."

I laughed at him. "I tell you you're a father and you're afraid that showing me a few light fixtures is going to scare me off?"

He immediately saw the humor. "Well, there's three hundred of them, it might be a bit daunting."

He opened the glass door to the terrace, and we stepped outside. The night was warm for November. Typical Los Angeles weather, unpredictable and extreme. I was so enamored with the view I didn't see the man dressed in a pair of jeans and a polo shirt walk out to join us.

"Oh, Michael," Sinclair said casually as he turned to the man.

"Mr. Harris." Michael was dressed as he belonged at a polo club, but was this his butler?

"Can you get a glass of chardonnay for my date and I'll have a Grey Goose Martini." His voice was warm, but commanding.

"Right away." Michael bowed as he turned and walk away.

"I was half expecting him to wear a tuxedo and speak with a British accent." I laughed.

"Oh, who wants to work in a tuxedo? I have the staff dress up if we're having guests, but I thought formal attire might put you off." He turned to me, looking sexy and commanding.

"I probably would have freaked a little, you're right." My heart was beating so hard, I thought he might see it pumping through the dress.

"Yeah, I figured. I'm not Batman. I don't live here alone with a grandfatherly, tuxedo-clad servant and cool gadgety stuff in the basement. I don't save the world. I just make movies. I like my staff to be happy. Happiness makes people more productive. That tip for success I learned early on." His eyes gleamed in the moonlight.

I almost lost track of what he was saying. When we first met I was amazed by his gigantic wings and toned six-pack. He was ethereal and rugged. As he stood in the moonlight, his eyes sparkling, I finally saw the real him. The man who wasn't hiding behind a rough commanding exterior or pretending to be a character from his movie. The man standing before me was one who didn't fly off the handle when he met his one-night stand in his office and gave her a job. Found out he was a father and still brought her home. The man before me was an incredible person.

"So, what you're saying about your employees being happy is, you're really an evil overlord master-minding your minions?" I felt flirty and playful, so I teased.

"...and also a Daddy it turns out." His face broke into a heartfelt smile.

His butler brought us a bottle of Chardonnay in a silver frosted bucket and a martini glass. He set the glass on the table, opened the bottle of wine, and poured a little.

"Would you like to sample the wine first, Miss?" He handed me a glass and offered me a taste.

"I'm sure it's delicious," I commented as I took a sip of the cooled wine with a deep citrus bite. As expected it was perfect. "I love it." I gave him a warm smile as he filled my glass.

"Enjoy your evening. Let me know when I can get either of you anything else." With that, he turned to leave.

"Thanks, Michael," I said as he walked into the house.

Sinclair picked up his glass and raised it to the air. "To us," he said plainly as he chinked his glass to mine.

I was finally feeling a little more relaxed. "This is heaven." I wasn't sure why I was so comfortable, we were still wading in treacherous uncharted waters.

"It is. You are so remarkably beautiful when you smile. I wish you'd do it more often." He slid in behind me and kissed my neck, martini glass in hand. "You're often so serious."

"Well, my boss puts a lot of pressure on me." I wiggled my ass on his cock to make a point. It was so hard and felt just right against my ass cheek.

He laughed and moved his hand around to my stomach and pressed himself against me.

"You're a very efficient and capable assistant. I doubt your boss is that demanding." He gave my ass a gentle thrust as he sipped his martini. "Have you always wanted to be an assistant?"

"Oh God, no," I blurted out. "I mean… Why no, not always." I shifted my voice to sound more regal… playing.

He laughed, and his chest and cock vibrated against my backside. "Being an assistant is that bad, huh? Tell me then, what do you want to be when you grow up, Reyna?"

"Being raised on a farm, the animals didn't feed themselves. I got up early and had a lot to do before I was free to do anything I wanted. I became good at being fast and efficient.

That's why being an assistant was a logical choice. While I was doing mundane tasks, though, I let my mind wander. I'd create stories in my head and write them down. So, I'm secretly a screenwriter."

"How Hollywood," he remarked with a note of sarcasm as his hand began to course slowly up my body.

The feeling of his hand and cock through the thin silk material of the dress was making me crazy. I took a sip of my wine and moaned a little leaning my head back onto his as his hand traveled dangerously near my breasts.

"I just optioned a script to the Fungus Film Lab, so we'll see where that leads."

His hand stopped just as he was cupping my left breast. "That's a great little indie production house. What's the film about?" He grazed his finger over my nipple, and I breathed in.

"It's about a little troll that wants to be a giant. He sets out to defeat a massive giant plaguing his village and ends up befriending him. The twist is, the giant has a learning disability, and that's why he'd been so mean to villagers and other trolls. It's a cute, feel-good film… and it's funny. I was inspired while I was pregnant with Arianna, thinking of all she might face being raised by a single mom. I loved the little troll idea… everyone is a giant in their own way. I have other films, but a friend of mine hooked me up with Fungus." I hoped he didn't mind discussing my film, but I loved talking about the stories I'd written or was planning to write. "I have a love story, Gothic, paranormal… fun."

He was driving me so crazy with his hand that it was hard to concentrate. His fingers smoothed over my nipple and back and forth until his hand glided down my body and rested on my hip.

"I'd like to read it…" His breath was hot in my ear.

"Sure." I bit my lip as I felt heat swelling between my legs. He was getting me so aroused.

"Put it in my reading box on Monday, or you're fired." His tongue wet the inside of my ear, and I felt myself gush a little.

Him wanting to read my screenplay, looking out at the city below like royalty, and his curious hand… I was losing it.

"I love the little troll idea. Too bad I didn't get it first. You talk like a true screenwriter; passionate about your work. And if it's even humanly possible, you're even sexier when you talk about your work. So… sex first or dinner? I know it's already pretty late, you must be starving." He took a sip of his martini, set it on the table, and traced my lip with his chilled thumb.

"You're hard to resist." I stared into his amazing green eyes and felt the connection between us tighten.

"I'm trying to be; I'm glad it's working." His finger traveled from my lip to my chin.

He planted a light kiss on my lips and thrust his pelvis forward, again I felt his needy cock.

"My bedroom is there." He turned me around and opened a set of French doors.

He opened the doors and revealed a stunning master suite. At the center was a king-sized bed draped in a soft steel gray fabric. On either side of the bed were brushed metal bedside tables and at the right corner was a sitting room and a master bathroom.

As soon as Sinclair entered the room, he removed his shoes, so I did the same.

"Well here's where all the magic happens." His voice was

thick and heady as he stalked towards me. "I plan to have you over and over again." The look on his face was sexually deviant; we were playing again.

"Perhaps I'll have you," I countered as I grabbed him and threw him down onto the bed.

"That works too." He laughed.

Chapter 15

Sinclair

She pushed me onto the bed and straddled my middle as she lifted my shirt. "Arms up," she commanded, and I obeyed, delighted she was taking charge.

I liked strong women; they were challenging. I'd let her take the lead for a while and then I'd turn the tables on her and send her to the moon. She was my goddess, and I planned on being her god. As soon as my chest was bared before her, she dipped her perfect body towards mine and claimed my lips. Her mouth was warm and sweet. She let her legs drape apart and cradle my steely cock between her thighs.

My hands caressed her ass and rode her silky dress up higher and higher until it was bunched under her breasts. As her mouth danced upon mine, my hands slid up to find she was wearing quite a substantial bra.

"What's with the armor?" I rasped into her mouth.

She wiggled herself on my engorged cock more. "I have a kiddo to feed. I thought the dress looked better without milk stains on my tits."

I almost flipped her under me and fucked her senseless, snarky little vixen. I didn't want to destroy this slow burn, and yet,

I had to be inside of her. She was too much. She ground herself on me, creating a mind whirling friction, scrambling my brain.

Her mouth parted from mine, and she sat on me, driving my clothed cock up into her warm cavern as she swiped her dress over her shoulders. Her bra was formidable, but her nimble fingers danced around behind her and released her full, erect tits. Wow, they had grown. They were delightfully thick and round. My hands grabbed for them, and she stopped me, kissing my knuckles.

"They're full of milk." Her face reddened some with what I assumed was an embarrassment.

Right, of course, her breasts would be engorged; she was breastfeeding our kiddo.

"Does our daughter need milk? Should we do something?" I asked, being clueless about these things.

At the mention of the word, "our daughter," my heart stopped for a moment. The enormity of a "daughter" still too daunting to tackle.

"She's got plenty." Reyna's beautiful smile returned. "But I'm not sure you want it, so I think these might be off-limits until I can pump." She was playfully smug.

"I've waited too long for them, so I'll help you. Whatever you need. I just want to get them as soon as I can." I wasn't sure what I was getting myself into, but I was ready for it, and more than ready for her.

"Are you serious?" she asked, surprised.

"I think so, yeah." Why not?

"Well, since you're um… more dressed than I am. Can you go into the foyer and get my bag? There's a breast pump in there."

Oh, okay… I could easily say breast pumps were a first in my sexual life. I was game; why not? Her breasts being so full was fifty percent my fault, so I'd help her pump.

"No problem. Wait here. Why don't you make yourself more comfortable while I'm gone? I love those panties you're wearing, dear. I'd like them better, though, if they were on the floor and not on you." I looked at her with dark seduction.

This made her giggle as she stood up and wiggled her way out of them.

"Like this?" she asked as she lifted her hand above her head, dangling her panties between her fingers.

Standing before me, bare from head to toe, her beautiful body was perfectly silhouetted in the low light. She was the most beautiful thing I'd ever seen. Her form had changed. Having a baby had given her more curves and a rounded stomach. My groin was pulsating with desire. The most remarkable change, however, was the long thin line drawn across her lower abdomen. She'd had a C-section, and there was a demure scar still a pinkish red. Her battle wound for the effort of birthing our child. She seemed a little worried to reveal the new her, but she kept a brave face.

She dropped her panties to the ground. "Happy?"

"I will be," I growled as I left. "God, you're gorgeous. Get ready; I'm gonna love every inch of you when I return." A smile lit across her face, her fears evaporating before me.

Michael had set her things in the spare bedroom as I'd instructed. I found her bag and finally understood why she carried such a large one. Inside were diapers, bottles, a set of little clothes with tiny butterflies on them. My heart melted. Also, there was a nondescript black sack inside which I assumed was her pump. Not wanting to be caught rummaging through her things I brought the whole bag back to my bedroom. She was waiting for me on the bed, lounging on a large pillow with her legs casually spread.

She sat up as soon as I entered the room. "I'll take that," she said, getting off the bed.

I set the bag on the table and let her retrieve the pump. "This will take about twenty minutes, sorry."

"For feeding our child? Why on earth would a mother ever feel sorry about that?" I hated that her confidence was waning.

She had to know how beautiful she was and what a remarkable thing she'd done giving birth.

"It's just... I feel a little like a cow on the farm." Her eyes met mine, and then I saw the honesty in them.

"Nature is nature. We rutted like monkeys in the zoo before all of this pumping business." I wrapped my arms around her and kissed her soft neck.

I smelled the lingering scent of her perfume there and the heat of her arousal. "You sure you don't want my help? I'd be glad to assist in any way I can." I eyed her enormous breasts and just imagined massaging them as they expressed milk, the sustenance for our child.

"It's kind of gruesome." She bit her lip, and I held her tighter.

"I seriously doubt it. At least let me hold you while you do it." I nibbled at her neck, and she sucked in air. "Take your time. I'm just gonna love on you while you milk those fabulous tits."

"You really want to help?" She took the pump out and brought two cups and the machine over to the bed.

She made herself comfortable, and I snuck in behind her.

"Yep. I want to help. Show me what to do." This was starting to be fun.

"Well, these go on here." She suctioned the plastic cup to her breast and turned the machine on. It was a little milking machine, pulling at her tit and expressing milk from it. I felt the heat of her embarrassment.

"You don't have to watch this." Her face was flushed red.

"Okay. I won't watch." I kissed her neck. "How about I help with this one. I see you have another pump here."

"It'll make it go faster, I guess." She was finally conceding.

"Great, show me how it works." She took the pump out and did the same thing, suctioned it to her breast and turned it on. "All you have to do is hold it. The pump does the rest."

"Darn." I pretended to pout. "They look fun to play with." I gave her breast a little squeeze.

"Um unless you want to have milk all over the sheets, I'd keep the playing to a minimum." She settled into my arms while the pumps worked on her breasts.

While she pumped, I nuzzled her hair, kissed her neck, and earlobe. After a while, I talked a little dirty talk, telling her how I was going to suck on her pussy until she filled my mouth with another kind of milk. She laughed and tried to concentrate on what she was doing, but I was a marvelous distraction.

After twenty minutes, she was done.

"Good job," she congratulated me and put everything away.

As she was packing stuff back up, I took off my clothes. When she returned to bed, I was as naked as she was. My hand lazily stroked my cock, keeping it at attention for her return.

"Do you need help with that?" she asked in much the same manner I'd asked to help her pump her breasts. "I could go get the pump again." She had a devilish glint in her eye.

"Oh, heavens, no. I'm pretty good to go here," I teased. "All I need is you and that glorious pussy of yours."

"Are you sure? Everyone can use a helping hand from time to time." Her hand moved over mine and lovingly pumped up and down my engorged shaft.

All my cock wanted was her. I kissed the top of her head, letting my hand drop to my side. I just enjoyed the feel of her skin on mine. After a few gentle strokes, her warm mouth came down over the tip of my cock. Her hot tongue swirled and lapped up the lubricant dribbling out. My balls tightened under her expert care. It wouldn't take much to make me blow. If she deep throated me, I'd be a goner.

I propped myself up on my elbows. "I'm really ready for you, love," I said, encouraging her to move on before I shot cum in her mouth.

She licked down my shaft and gave my balls a sweet kiss.

"Are these mine now?" I asked, moving my fingers over her nipples, touching the tender areolas.

She presented her beautiful breasts to me. "Do what you will, sir. They're all yours."

I massaged her wonderfully soft tits for a minute before I leaned into her and popped one in my mouth. I could taste the sweet milk still lingering on it, so I sucked hard. It was only a taste, enough to understand what breasts were really for.

"Oh," she moaned, "my God." Her voice was ragged and aroused.

She must've been sensitive after pumping. I swirled my tongue around the tender bud before moving on to the next. I was quite impressed with how well she had recovered from having a baby. The baby weight barely showed, and where there was a little extra softness, it only made her more sensuous.

I enjoyed exploring her new curves. While I'd only seen her body once before, I loved the subtle changes motherhood had given her. I worked my way down to the long scar across her belly where our child was brought into the world. The thin deep pink line looked proud and perfect, the remnants of a harrowing night. I kissed her round belly focusing on her belly button as she squirmed.

"My body has changed a lot," she confessed as if it was some sort of crime to have given birth.

"I was just thinking about how much I love this part." My voice glided over her soft skin as I extended my tongue to taste the painful scar.

Her body arched, and she let out a graveled groan.

"Does it hurt?" I stopped for a moment.

"No, it's just… it… feels weird." I wasn't sure she liked my licking her scar, but she didn't seem to hate it. "Shall I continue or ease on down the road?"

"Continue." Her breath was throaty and impassioned.

"Well, then. I love every inch of you." I kissed her scar before I descended to graze my stubbled chin across her pelvic bone.

"Arraaahh." She was so amazingly responsive.

I saw the sacrifices her body gave to produce our child. Sacrifices she'd born alone. I lavished her with my attention, neglecting the pounding throb of my cock, to celebrate her and the ultimate gift of womanhood. My poor penis had ballooned up to its full size. With it's mushroom head pulsing, dribbling pre-cum down the shaft, it was hard to focus on anything else. It'd have to settle down. This moment was all about her, my goddess. My goal was to have her fully satisfied and begging before I entered her.

I dipped my face into the heaven between her legs. My tongue traced the tender pink skin surrounding her vagina as she gently bucked into my mouth. My tongue slid along her delicious slit until it found her swelling clit, hiding behind its hood. I nibbled and sucked at the soft sweet spot until I heard her begin to pant. Her juices flowed into my mouth, and I knew she was climbing towards a climax. Her breathing hitched as her body pulsed into mine. I kissed her clit and looked up at her across the valley of her body.

"Come on, baby," My voice was a deep purr, "Cum for me."

Her eyelids fluttered as she moaned, and I slid my fingers into her wet center, while my tongue continued to play on her clit. Her hips bucked and rolled. She gritted her teeth, trying to hold back her scream. I dove another finger into her and pumped them harder. That was all she needed. Riding the tide of her orgasm, her hips shook, and her pelvis quivered on my mouth, gushing her arousal.

"That's a girl," I praised as I slathered her pussy with her thick release.

I kissed the tuft of hair at the top of her mound and slithered my way up her flushed skin as she shivered and cooled from her incredible orgasm.

"Oh, my God," she whispered again as I made my way up to her mouth to claim her lips, the taste of her still on me.

My rock hard cock was lodged between us as I used my hands to spread her wider to accommodate my enlarged size.

"Are you ready for me?" I asked as I smoothed damp strands of hair from her face.

"I'm so ready for you," she panted.

I rubbed my cock head up and down her slit, stimulating more lubrication, so she didn't feel any pain upon entry. When I knew she was good and wet, I positioned my throbbing cock at her entrance.

Before I dove into the bliss between her legs, I asked. "Are you on the pill?" I knew it would break the mood some, but we were already surprised with one child, I don't think we were ready for another now… or ever.

"Yes, you're good to go." She gave me a reassuring smile as her hips jutted up to meet mine.

She attempted to impale herself on me from underneath but did nothing more than knock my desperate cock with her wet center, driving me madder.

"Okay, then… here we go." I used my hand to guide my cock to her pussy.

My pre-cum mixed with her juices created the perfect viscosity. I slid in as gently as her tight pussy allowed. She squealed, and her body arched, which panicked me some.

"Am I hurting you?" I asked, worried that I may have impaled something sore within her.

"Just a little achy, but in a good way. We're good, I'm good… it's all good." In her ecstasy she was blathering a bit, it was so cute and aroused me more.

I loved seeing her so dazed and euphoric. Her pussy hugged my cock like a glove. I slid in and out of her to a slow rhythm like an exquisite dance. I was made for her body. The smile on her face illustrated for me how right we were. She lifted her legs into the air to allow more of me inside of her. Her eyes closed, and she gritted her teeth when I pressed deeper into her.

"You still all good?" I checked in.

"Yes… just fuck me, Sinclair," she rasped.

"Well, alright then." I laughed.

My arousal could no longer be controlled anyway, so with her permission, I pumped in and out of her as hard and fast as our bodies could go. My fingers dove to her clit as my cock slammed against her soft skin. My balls bounced back and forth, and my stomach wound in knots, spiraling towards a massive climax.

I'd been without her for too long, and my need for her was monumental. I pumped in, and as she mewled, whimpering with desire, coming closer to another release of her own, it was all I could take. I leaned forward and pressed myself as deep into her as my cock would fit. Feeling her body enveloping mine, I shot load after load of cum into her soft, warm core. Her legs wrapped around me, holding me deep within as she cried out in ecstasy. Her pussy clenched my penis while it quivered under me. Moments later, she found her own release as it warmed my cock.

"Fuck," I exhaled as I jettisoned the last of my

cum into her.

She was the most amazing lover. I didn't want to withdraw from her body. I wanted to stay seated in her forever. I stayed inside her for a while longer, enjoying the wetness of our combined release dribbling down my thigh. I rolled her on top of me, her legs drifting to either side of my body. She was totally spent as her hot forehead rested on my chest.

"Thank you," she sighed, and I felt her stomach heave breaths on mine.

"There's much more where that came from," I teased giving her sweet bare ass a playful slap.

The shock of my hand on her ass caused her body to jut forward, and my cock dislodged, dripping and sated.

I cradled her body in my arms while my hands stroked her warm skin. We stayed there for a while, holding one another until our passions had cooled and we were left feeling rather sticky.

"How about we have a shower and then dinner? I'm starving," I whispered in her ear.

"Perfect." She kissed me.

"We'll be doing much more of this later," I told her as I lifted her from the bed and carried her to the bathroom.

We had a quick shower, being too tired and hungry to do anything other than soap up and rinse off. I was looking forward to dinner as I had something very special planned.

Chapter 16

Reyna

He was an exquisite lover and celebrated my body with such care. I was worried that after having Ariana, he might think I wasn't as attractive anymore. I certainly didn't have the same body after the baby, but I liked my new curves. Luckily, he did too.

After we showered, I put some comfortable clothes on. The premiere started at sundown; the party began around six-thirty, and now it was already nine o'clock at night. I needed to check in with Melody and Charlynn and see how Arianna was doing. I felt guilty I didn't call sooner, but they told me not to call at all. So, waiting as long as I did, was really quite a feat. I hadn't ever been away from my baby this long. I loved being with Sinclair and enjoyed getting to know him more intimately, but I missed my baby girl.

Melody answered on the first ring, "Nine o'clock. I'm impressed, Reyna. Arianna is a perfect angel. She's had her bottles, burped, had a bath. We sang to her, and she fell right to sleep. I'm taking the first shift, and Charlynn has the second… and you're not to call again. We'll call you if there's an issue, but I want you to enjoy your night, morning, and another night if you want it." She said most of all of it in one breath.

"Hello." I laughed.

"Oh, and did I tell you, we love your baby?" She also laughed.

"It seems like it. So all's well, I can run off to Paris now?" I teased.

"Yep, we'll raise your perfect baby," she said without

missing a beat.

No matter how great they were being about taking care of her, I still missed her like crazy. Even teasing about someone else caring for her for the long term struck a chord deep inside of me. I felt a little pang, even though I knew nothing could separate us.

"So. how is it going?" She dropped her voice to a whisper.

"It's going great. Sinclair is amazing." I wanted to tell her all the overwhelming things I was thinking, but it wasn't the right time for that.

There was such a warm love brewing between Sinclair and me; however, Melody had been really hurt recently. Her Halloween night last year didn't go well at all. She had fun playing her music, and later that evening she did meet an actor. He'd been in a few recognizable movies. He was so hot and dreamy, and after the party, they dated for a while. She fell hard for him, and he was basically an asshole. I think she even thought he might be the one. She wanted a family and children. She was even more eager for them than I was. I understood how painful breakups were.

Just after she got dumped, I found out I was pregnant. I was worried about being a single mom and raising Arianna alone. Melody and Charlynn assured me they'd be there for me every step of the way, and they had been. I think Arianna helped Melody as much as she helped me. Being her auntie was helping Melody heal from the breakup. Charlynn's year wasn't much better than Melody's, so being able to spend the night with Arianna and love on her sweetness was good for both of my dear roommates.

"I'm so happy for you, Rey. Don't worry about us. We are so good; you just go back to him and have the night of your life. And I mean it, if you want to stay another night, just let us know. Charlynn and I are both good with it." She was so sweet and encouraging.

"I'm pretty sure I'll be home. I miss my baby and um… you know what they say about too much of a good thing." I dropped my voice so Sinclair couldn't hear me, even though he was in the bathroom getting dressed. "I want him to work for it a little." I laughed.

"Oh, yes, you do. Okay, we'll see you tomorrow. Love you!" she said as I heard Charlynn with Arianna in the background cooing and singing.

She must have woken up. "Love you too, and thanks again. Bye."

"Bye," she said before she hung up and Sinclair walked out of the bathroom looking clean and refreshed.

He was wearing a soft pair of jogging pants and another cotton T-shirt. I had on a short summer dress.

"You look beautiful," he mentioned as he strolled over to me… all alpha man, strong and commanding.

"So do you," I said as my face flushed, thinking of his body and the amazing sex we'd just had.

His hands snaked around me as he drew me up to his chest, angled my head back, and opened his mouth to kiss me. His kiss was ardent and hard. I kept up with his passion and thought he might throw me on the bed and take me, despite how hungry I was. Instead, he lifted my dress and looked at my lace underwear.

"These are lovely," he mentioned as his fingers slid them off.

"Hey, I'm starving horny boy, can we save the bed gymnastics for after dinner?" I loved exploring sex with him, but I needed to eat.

"Yep, just want you ready for me when we do," he said as he neatly placed my underwear on the dresser.

"And what about you, Mr. 'Let's not wear our panties to dinner.' I sure hope you aren't…" I jabbed my hand to his cock and found it hard and easily defined through the thin, soft pant material. "Never mind, you aren't wearing any either are you?" I blushed.

"You make me crazy; I thought it'd be best I have easy access…" He laughed as he pulled away from me and grabbed my hand to follow him. "Let's eat."

I had to tell my legs to walk, as they suddenly turned to rubber. I hadn't realized when we were on the terrace that the house was such a twirling maze. There were different levels and rooms. The architecture was sort of as whacky as the office. I had no clue where we were exactly. We exited his room into a hallway. We passed several other rooms, most of them were guest bedrooms, and then we were out into the main living room again. We walked down a long set of stairs to the kitchen.

"I thought since it was just the two of us we'd eat in my favorite spot. There's a formal dining room on the main floor, but I rarely eat in there," he confessed. "My mom and dad used to throw these huge parties, but I'm not much of a party at home kind of guy." He turned to me seductively. "I like it to be just one on one."

"Or one under one, as the case may be." I smiled as I playfully jabbed his shoulder.

"Very true in our case." He led me to a small den.

I smelled something amazing. We followed the scent to an

outdoor room. It was entirely enclosed in glass, even the ceiling. We were surrounded by trees and large rocks, and in the middle of the room was a table.

"Wow." The space mystified me.

You couldn't see the road or the other houses, just nature, and an incredible view of the valley below. The mansion was tucked into the Hollywood Hills. No one would ever see us because there were no other houses around, and the terrain was too treacherous to climb.

"I love this room," he said as he pulled a chair out for me.

I sat down, and he sat next to me. "I love it too. It's like we're completely away from the world."

"It feels that way, doesn't it? Sometimes you can see animals at night. Usually just skunks and raccoon, but there's larger stuff too like a coyote or the occasional bobcat."

"Really? Bobcats? That's amazing." I barely believed him, but I'd heard we had such animals in the hills.

"I've seen two… or perhaps, one twice. It is amazing, truly magical." He seemed like a child, filled with wonder. "I designed this room, especially for viewing nature. It was one of the rooms I had added to the original structure. I wanted to have a place where I could escape from the world," he said as Michael entered carrying two glasses, his martini, and my wine.

He set my wine before me. "Thanks, Michael," I chirped, probably sounding too eager.

Sinclair nodded to Michael when he set the martini glass down. "We'll have the appetizer now." He was very formal with the butler.

He may have let him wear casual clothes, but there was nothing casual about their relationship. It wasn't anything like the relationship I had with my roommates. I'd think it would be lonely living in this huge house with servants who just treated you like a god and nothing more.

As soon as Michael left, I asked, "How long has he been working for you?"

"Michael worked with my parents before I took over the house, so it's been something like seven years, I think." He took a sip of his drink.

"Seven years and you two aren't bros?" If I was going to do this with him, then I had to be myself. I wouldn't be his assistant in bed or in our private life. I was his equal. I treated him as I would a friend and lover, not a boss who had a shit ton of money and power.

He almost spat out his drink. "No, I wouldn't call Michael and me bros exactly. I have brothers; I'm bros with them… or rather one of them." He sipped his drink again, looking a little off-color.

"Well, you should chill with Michael. You can never have too many friends," I instructed as I drank my wine.

"Being friends with help can be dangerous." His eyes were dark and penetrating.

"Not being friends with the people who work in your home can be dangerous." I returned his glare in a playful way. "You're a pretty dark and brooding guy at times, aren't you? The Dark One, mysterious lover, fallen angel movies, the omnipresent boss at work, yet with perks like a basketball court and get fucked Fridays. Deep down, you're a little sinister." I was being an armchair psychiatrist, but his lack of chill was starting to bother me.

"Bingo. Actually, I'm just a little cynical. I wouldn't go so far as to diagnose me as a Sith Lord just yet, but I have my brooding side. I don't have a red room of pain; however, I do have a blue room of horror. I'd love to show it to you one day." Michael returned with a platter of fruit, bread, and cheeses, and Sinclair eyed him, considering their "bro" status perhaps.

"Oh, my favorite!" I exclaimed looking at the food and trying to ignore the weird confession he'd just made. "My roommates and I have fancy finger food days at least once a month," I blurted out, not realizing how pedestrian it might have made me sound.

"You told me you were a vegetarian, so I made sure Salvatore created some exquisite vegetarian offerings to tempt your pallet. Trust me; it will be a celebration for your mouth." Ugh, more highbrow from him.

"I'm excited." I waited for him to serve me a plate of food as I didn't want to appear too starving, even though I was. I figured I'd play a damsel in distress or whatever he wanted me to be for a while if I could get him to lighten up in return. "Looks amazing." I picked up a glossy green olive dusted with spices and popped it in my mouth. "So this horror room…" I finally mentioned with the olive bobbing. "Is it like a dungeon kinda thing? 'Cause I'm just going to tell you now I don't do whips and chains. If you have abuse issues, I'll give you my therapist's phone number, not my ass." I smiled, hoping he didn't weird out on me.

He burst out with a genuine laugh. "As right as you should. No, it's a room full of horror memorabilia and nerdy stuff. It's just off the theater I built into the basement. "I mean chains are fun… I like them, but no whips. Life is painful enough." He finished filling his plate.

There it was, "life is painful enough." Actually, life wasn't that painful for most people and certainly not for him. I wonder why he thought it was.

"When you say you like chains, you mean?" I gave him the side-eye, trying to draw him out more.

"I mean I like them… for me. Sometimes I want to be… bound. A little cock torture can be fun…" He actually said that. "And… I use them in the theater to lock guests in the chairs so they'll watch my movies. I may just make you watch a few of my film school firsts if you don't behave." His voice was finally playful, yet still sinister, crazy man.

"Oh no… please, Master, no!" I tried my best to amp up the histrionics. "So… you like to be bound? I'll file that away in a safe place. I'm sure I could find some cock torture tutorials on YouTube." I leered and picked up a tiny bite-sized carrot and bit down hard.

"Oh no you won't…" he leered back. "They won't be on YouTube, that's for sure. Unless you want medical grade instruction. I'd say you'd have to dig a little deeper in the dark recesses of the web to find what I like… but not too deep. I enjoy a little titillating, but not brutalization. Why are we talking about this?" He was suddenly uncomfortable.

"Your horror room set you off on this little tangent, my friend, but since I left my catsuit and whips at home, your cock is safe. I still have my breast pump, though." I looked at him with a gleam in my eye.

"Nope, nope, and nope… and if we talk any more about this, I'll spread you out on this table and feast on you. Then, Michael and I will have an awful lot of bro stuff to talk about," he said as he licked an oyster out of the shell and swallowed it.

I burst out into laughter. "There's the fun side of you," I announced.

"Oh, I'm plenty of fun, just you wait."

The rest of dinner was delightful. He was right; the vegetarian food was perfect and delicious. I couldn't wait to go back to his bedroom and torture his cock, but he had other plans for us. As soon as we were finished with our meal, it was nearly eleven-thirty at night. Michael came in and bid his farewell for the evening. We said our goodbyes, and he left.

I was worried he might live in the house near our bedroom and Sinclair assured me that Michael and Lorna, his wife, the housekeeper, lived in a house on his property farther up the hill. Apparently, the two of them had worked for his parents. They were in their early fifties, didn't have kids, and Sinclair assumed didn't want any. Their only job was to attend Sinclair, who was rarely there. He noted they had a sweet gig.

After Michael left, Sinclair turned to me with the devil in his eye.

"Oh... now," I said with a nervous tinge to my voice. "I'm getting to know that look. What have you got planned, Sin?" I used his nickname as he seemed more like the character he pretended to be on Halloween than the bossy boss I worked for and now dated.

"I was thinking I might just feast on you as I mentioned." His face seemed deadly serious even though I hoped he was playing.

"Oh?" My voice was mostly a yelp.

I was completely full and really couldn't jump back into sex right away without getting a stomach cramp. I was pretty sure the same rules applied to bump and grind as they did for swimming.

"Aren't you full from dinner? I know I sure am." I stood up from the table and backed away from him some, giving chase.

He laughed, seeing the game I'd started. "I always have room for you." He slunk forward as I planned my escape.

There weren't many doors in the room, only the one we entered from and one leading outside. Unsure of what I'd find behind either door, I opted to go outside since that door was the closest. I hadn't much time. I moved a chair between us, giving me only a second to unlock it and slip outside. The air was crisp, but not too cold. I felt the draft on my bare pussy, which aroused me as did the fact that he'd slipped out right behind me and seized my waist.

"Not the smartest idea to run from a man in his own home." He laughed as he held me tightly against him.

I wiggled and bucked trying to get out of his grip as one hand dipped from my waist to my wet pussy. His fingers rubbed across my clit, fast and ferocious as he held me to him with a vice-like grip. His fingers were relentless, yet he remained calm. He kissed my neck and shoulders, intermittently biting. It wasn't long before he had me convulsing on him as a powerful orgasm rocked my whole body. He withdrew his finger and licked my arousal off of it.

"The appetizer," his graveled voice announced.

I was drifting down from my release feeling dazed. The moon was high above and shone a beautiful light on us. To the right was a magnificent waterfall which flowed into a hot tub carved into the rock. It had a distinctly Asian feel with the natural setting and the simple architectural lines. A wooden platform surrounded the hot tub, and small metal lanterns lit the path.

He guided me, still limp and sated, to one of the many benches surrounding the tub. "This is my sanctuary," he whispered in my ear as he seated me in his lap, spreading my legs over his.

He opened me wide before him, baring my ravaged pussy to the cool night air.

"It's beautiful," I said as I tried to close my legs out of modesty.

He lightly scolded, "Ah, ah, ah, I'm not done yet," he chided, drawing my thighs apart with his knees.

He used one hand to keep me open, and the other dipped into my vagina. Ribbons of steam coursed into the air from the deep warm pool and everything smelled like cedar and eucalyptus. My head was spinning as his fingers dipped in and out of me, painting my pussy with my cum. The more I wiggled, the deeper his finger dove. He added another finger in while his other hand pinched and pulled at my nipple, bringing my milk down. My mind was a swirling erotic mess.

Chapter 17

Sinclair

I wanted to give her pleasure and experiences she'd only dreamed of. As she was spread before me on the bench, she almost came again, but I didn't want her too spent. So I lifted her to her feet and removed her dress in one sweeping motion, leaving her standing there naked in the moonlight, gloriously beautiful.

She turned to me and glared, "And what about you? Are you just going to stand there with your clothes on while I'm all Lady Godiva here?" She pretended to pout.

Her face, flushed with ecstasy, was too tempting to resist. As turnaround was fair play, I gave her a shot at me. I spread my arms wide. "You're certainly welcome to undress me."

"Oh, buddy I will." She turned to me and lifted my T-shirt up, trying to get it over my head, being almost a foot shorter than me. I let her struggle for a moment, then pulled it the rest of the way off and tossed it on the bench.

"I love these," she cooed caressing my pectoral muscles.

"And I love these," I added kneading her breasts.

Her hands danced down my body until they came to rest in my pants, her fingertips tickling the hair around my rock hardness. She quickly released my cock from my pants, and I chucked them off. She proceeded to kiss her way down my body until she came face to face with my cock. Before going further, her hands traced the outline of my tattoo.

"So," she started, looking up from my rising member, "I've been curious about this," she said as she continued to course her fingers over the Gothic cross. "Is it a Jesus complex? Tramp stamp? A drunken night out with the boys?"

"A little bit of all that." I touched her silky, soft hair. "…and a reminder. To behave." Her innocent face shone in the moonlight.

If I dared to walk down this path with her, I had to tread lightly. She was the mother of our child, a goddess, a muse, and I was slipping too quickly into her abyss.

"What do you mean, behave?" Her face looked a bit worried.

I hadn't told her about the tattoo; there wasn't a good time. I'd gotten it when I was drunk with the boys, yes. And it was to celebrate my manhood, true, but there was a deeper meaning I'd never shared. I was honest when I said it was to remind me to behave. In college, I'd had a taste of freedom. No longer under the strict rule of my parents and released to exercise my demons, I unleashed the worst. I'd slept with so many young, beautiful, college women. All were eager to throw off their own chains, and I took advantage of them.

I let my cock rule everything for about a year. I reasoned if they wanted me, then I had no responsibility for their actions or mine. The truth was, I took no responsibility at all. Regretfully, Reyna's child was not the first I'd fathered. When I was a freshman in college, the woman I'd been dating for a couple of months came to me and told me she was pregnant. For a few days, I completely freaked. I was going to be a father, and I'd had to give up everything… all my hopes and dreams. I didn't even think about her and what she'd have to sacrifice.

When she told me a month later she'd decided to end the pregnancy, I felt a mix of relief and a weird disappointment. I wasn't ready to be a father, and I realized I didn't want to be one, at least not then. She and I parted ways. I only saw her occasionally on campus. When I did see her, I'd think she had my child growing in her, and we let that baby go. We passed each other and say nothing to one another… virtual strangers.

I got the tattoo on a drunken whim. I told myself and my buddies it was to glorify my illustrious member. In truth, it was to remind me to behave. Strange, I found myself in the same situation, even with the stupid tattoo… and yet, not. As soon as I found out that Reyna had given birth to my child, I knew I'd be a better man than I was to the unfortunate woman whose name had escaped me.

"The tattoo helps remind me that sometimes, with sex comes great responsibility; don't abuse its power."

Her hand, which was gently stroking me, stopped for a moment. "Um… maybe it should have been bigger," she teased as she pumped me harder. "It takes two to tango. I knew what I was getting into. The tattoo's cool, though," she affirmed while her hands worked their magic.

Her hand moved up and down my shaft moving my foreskin, driving me absolutely wild. She continued to pump me harder and harder until that familiar knot formed in my groin. I grabbed her hand and stilled her assault.

"Wow," I rasped with desire. "Take it easy, turbo."

She bent down and planted a kiss on my cock. "Sorry big guy, I got carried away."

She then stood up, turned from me, showing off her perfect ass, and slunk over to the hot tub. Within moments, she submerged into the warm water. The little vixen left me standing there erect as she went into the pool without me.

"So you're just going to leave me here hanging?" I sulked.

"You are not hanging, sir. You are very pointy." She smiled her glorious grin as she dipped below the surface.

She was driving me insane. I walked to the tub and entered the water, scooping her up into my arms. "How's this for pointy?" I asked as I jutted my cock between her ass cheeks.

"Aye." She tried to move away as I positioned myself right at the entrance of her pussy.

She was trying not to put all of her weight down after I'd wiggled in under her. There was no escape, though. I pressed my cock between her ass cheeks and held her captive. Although she must have thought I was going to spear her and give her a quick fuck, I didn't. I simply held her with our bodies aligned. We stayed in the water for a while. I massaged her muscles and smoothed my hands over her skin... loving, exploring, caring.

"It feels natural having you here," I confessed, probably too soon.

"It does," was all she said as her head lilted onto my chest. Her eyes drifted closed. After a half-hour, I thought she might have fallen asleep, but she roused and started wiggling on my cock, which had wilted some. It flared back to life again pretty quickly as her ass squeezed and released it several times.

Her breasts had filled with milk again, but I massaged her tits, allowing her breast milk to dribble out and mix with the water.

"That feels good. They were getting achy." I was happy to give her some release.

Without saying a word, she angled her ass forward and pressed my aching cock into her pussy. She then sat her full weight down on me and began to ride me gently.

"Thank you," I groaned while she picked up her speed.

It was a little hard to get leverage with the buoyancy of the water, so I lifted us up to the edge of the tub, giving us more gravity. She moved forward, braced her hands on her knees, and fucked me hard. It was hypnotic, her tight pussy sucking at my cock up and down and stroking it rhythmically in the cool night air. My arms wrapped around her waist, driving my cock in deeper. After a while, it all became too much. I stood up with her still lodged on my dick and turned her toward the mountains. She braced herself on the rock wall as I fucked her doggy-style. My dick thrust hard into her as my balls slapped against her pussy.

She must have liked the rough fucking because she started mewling and whining, "Sinclair, oh my God, yes, yes... .go deeper." I was happy to see she was losing it as badly as I was.

I slammed my cock in as deep as it could go and found I'd reached the end of her love canal. She bucked a bit when I hit her cervix, but also screamed in ecstasy. That I was all I needed; I shattered and convulsed inside of her, filling her up with hard jets of sperm. I'd never cum so hard and so much with any other woman. Reyna was like a drug. She intoxicated me with her very essence. When I'd unloaded every drop I had, I pulled out of her and rested on the seat, my cock swollen and oozing the remnants of our passions.

"God, what you do to me." I could barely breathe as I tried to find order in the world again.

She said as she kissed me, "Don't forget it when we're back in the office on Monday." She flopped back into the water and let the warmth of it cascade around her.

I joined her in the water. "There is no way I'll ever forget this, or you, or any of what we're building. Monday is going to be my own personal hell; don't you worry," I assured her.

"Why?" She really had no idea what an effect she had on me.

"Because all I'll want to do is fuck you." I grinned.

"I hope one day you'll want to do more than that." She seemed sad, but I didn't have the energy to address it just yet.

I hadn't the strength to tell her I wanted everything, the whole package. The budding filmmaker, the mother of my child, the wife of my dreams... but it was all too soon and too much to lay on her so soon. I let the comment linger as we held one another in the moonlight.

After some time had passed, she spoke. "I like slumber parties at your house. I'm curious, though, is there going to be any sleeping happening? I'm getting really tired." She yawned.

"Come on, sleeping beauty." I lifted her into my arms. "Time for bed." With that, I carried her to my bedroom and placed her naked on the crisp white sheets.

She was asleep before her head even hit the pillow, and the love I had for her swelled... this certainly could be mine ever after.

Chapter 18

Reyna

I woke up just as dawn was breaking. I had been conditioned by Ariana to wake up early, so I missed her. However, it felt good to have Sinclair's warm, naked body up against mine. He had me cradled in his arms, and his semi-hard cock was on my ass. It felt right being held by him like this could be home one day. I didn't want to think too much about it. Sinclair and I were just getting to know one another.

I had to go to the bathroom and pump, so I snuck out of bed without rousing him. When I came back, he was sitting up working on his phone. He looked like a naked, busy businessman. As soon as he saw me standing there, he patted the bed beside him.

"Are you coming back?" He didn't even look up from his phone.

I jumped in the bed and snuggled in trying not to be irritated he was on his phone. "Do you need to work?" I asked, looking at his phone screen to see what he was doing.

"I'm just answering some emails. No one should ever work on the weekends, but apparently, everyone thinks I should. Is everything okay? You jumped out of bed so fast." He seemed a bit off like he was nervous for some reason.

"Yeah, everything's fine. I had to pump, and you know, do boring biological things. I do miss the little bug, though. I've never woke up without her." I didn't want to go, but I also didn't want to be away much longer.

"It must be hard for you to be away from her." He still

seemed a bit weird.

"It is, but I'm having fun with you." I gave him a reassuring smile; this seemed to make him happier.

"You think you have time for a quick tumble? And… I'm sure Lorna made breakfast already, if you're hungry, after. Perhaps you can come back tonight and bring Arianna?" He looked like a little boy, eyes big and hopeful.

I didn't want to dash his spirits, but I certainly wasn't ready to bring Arianna here. I was just getting to know Sinclair, and it was all overwhelming enough.

"Definitely someday," I said, kissing his forehead, "But not tonight. I should stay home tonight. Everything is kind of big and swirling in my brain right now. I need a little space to um… sort it all out." I kissed his shoulder and let my hand trace the muscles on his chest to ease the impact of my words.

"Are you having doubts?" The worry had returned to his voice.

"No silly." I slapped him. "I'm just not ready to fuck my boss, have a baby with him, and cohabitate all at once… I need to ease on down this road… you know." My hand slid down his stomach. "I've had an incredible time, though."

"Me too, and I don't think I'll let you go." He seized my hand, not knowing how creepy the gesture was.

Good thing I trusted him as much as I did. "That's a little creepy, in an 'I'm gonna kidnap you' kind of way," I teased.

"Well, if you put it that way, then by all means leave." He pouted.

Such a baby. I guess I had to prove I was in this all the

way. I drew back the sheet to reveal his cock jutting to the ceiling. "I see your problem. This thing here," I touched his cock, "needs some attention." He was so childish with his silly sulking.

"Whatever you can offer will be greatly appreciated," he said as his hands flanked my sides.

I straddled him and placed my pussy over his cock. "Since sir fucked my pussy so hard, I won't be able to sit at my desk on Monday. You're not getting any more of the love cavern until next time. But... a little cock torture might be in order." I pushed my pussy down on him and slid back and forth over his erection, pressing all my weight into the effort.

"Oh," he gasped, "Okay, this is good."

Rubbing on him was getting me wet. I really was too sore to have his thick cock inside of me, but this felt incredible. His shaft grazed up and down my clit, and I found myself getting flushed. My insides felt like the Fourth of July. I grounded down hard on him. His arms wrapped around me and held me in place as he moaned loudly. I pressed in harder bucking my hips back and forth until I felt him seize, hold me steadfast and shudder. His cock pulsed and spurt a stream of cum onto his chest. I milked his cock more as thick ribbons shot out. It pooled near his belly button then began to ooze down his sides onto the crumpled sheets below. He made small yelping sounds as he finished, and I collapsed down on him seeking my own release.

"My turn," I requested, kissing his lips.

He flipped me over, spread my legs, and dove his face into my pussy, our musk and pleasure still slick on my mound. He lapped it all up, then thrust his tongue inside me over and over. His tongue soothed my ravaged insides, and I found myself rolling into a sweet climax as I shuddered and flooded his mouth.

When we were done, he kissed my pussy, belly, and breasts, coming to rest on my mouth.

"What do you say? Shower, eat, and get you home?" He seemed sad but committed to doing the right thing.

"Sounds perfect." My hand caressed his stubbled face, loving his beautiful heart.

He was showing me so much respect that it was hard to resist, but I didn't want to burn us out too fast. Everything was already moving at the speed of light. I told myself it was fine if he was a one-night stand. I had a miracle gift I'd always treasure from that night. When I accepted the job working for him, I figured I'd use this time to get to know him and perhaps advance my career. When he wanted to pursue something more, I still thought it would be dating and a few fun nights, but what I was feeling now... the love, the adoration, and respect; that was a forever kind of feeling, and it scared me.

It frightened me because I doubted he was in the same lane. He was willing to honor the fact that he had a child, and I appreciated that; however, marriage, monogamy, fatherhood, he already said, he wasn't in for that. I had to go home to gain some distance again.

We ate a nice breakfast of fruit and muesli which had already been laid out for us.

"I have stuff that isn't so healthy if you want it. Lorna just knows what I like. She can make you anything."

"This is exactly what I wanted for breakfast," I said pouring myself a bowl of cereal.

After we ate, we showered, and he drove us in his Land Rover to my apartment.

When we got to my place, I kissed him and prepared to say goodbye… for now. "I had the best night. It was magical. Thank you," I said as I opened my door and stepped out of the car.

He seemed a bit panicked as he ran around the car to meet me. I was already marching up the steps to my apartment. Why I was running from him, I had no idea. Clearly, I had more issues with us than I cared to address.

"Woah, there." He took my hand gently, back to his commanding alpha self again. He looked down at the wrist he was grabbing and curled his fingers around my hand to hold it. "I'm not sure why you're running, love." His finger stroked my hand.

"Me either," I bowed my head.

"Can I see her? I won't if you don't want me to, but… I want…" He took a deep breath. "This is hard… I don't want to rush you or overstep. I'm an asshole, usually. I'd run from me too because if I were being me, I'd just follow you in. But, I want your permission. This is still your life."

I squeezed his hand and thought for a minute. "Sure. Come on in. Welcome to my crazy," I said as we walked up the stairs to my apartment. When we got to the door, I turned to him. "Just to warn you, my roommates will probably freak."

"Consider me warned." He smoothed his hand on my back. "Nothing really scares me."

I opened the door and walked in. Melody was playing guitar on the couch, and Charlynn was in the kitchen washing baby bottles. Shocked and awestruck, Melody stopped playing as soon as she saw Sinclair.

"I'm home," I announced as if I were on a television sitcom.

Melody just stared at Sinclair. I forgot how dashing he was. He did sort of stop traffic. Neither of my roommates had ever seen him, only heard me babble on about him. Of course, there was the legendary fucking from Halloween, they certainly knew all about that. Just before my date, I told them the truth about him.

"How was everything?" I asked to break the silence.

"She's a total dream. I love her. I love her," Melody gushed.

Charlynn yelled from the kitchen not turning from her dishes to look at us, "I love her too. Don't let Melody fool you into letting her babysit without me. Hey… aren't you supposed to be fucking the baby daddy? I thought we told you to stay the whole weekend," she scolded as she finished the last of the bottles.

Sinclair gave me a sweet glare and whispered, "I could have kept you all weekend? Hmmm."

Charlynn turned off the water. "What happened? He turned out to be a dud? Maybe he just needs a mask to get it up." When she turned around her mouth nearly hit the floor.

"Baby daddy's here." Sinclair smiled.

"Oh fuck," Charlynn gasped. She looked at him and giggled. "I'll just be right over in the corner chewing on my sandal. Guess it went well." She laughed, brushing off the incident.

"I'd say it did," Sinclair played along.

"No complaints here," I added, thoroughly embarrassed.

"I'll leave my number with you just in case. Maybe you can give me some pointers. I'm kind of useless without my mask." He was at ease and joking, so not the Sinclair I'd seen in the past.

"Oh my God, don't." I rolled my eyes.

"Is she awake?" I asked in a whisper thinking, she wasn't with them so was probably asleep.

"I just put her down," Melody said, mirroring my whisper.

"Okay, I'm just going to take baby daddy to meet his spawn." I raised my eyebrows, and everyone laughed.

"Hope there aren't any horns," he teased as he followed me into my bedroom.

He… Sinclair Harris, this formidable boss, and producer, was in my tiny Hollywood apartment chillin' with my kooky roommates and it all felt good. Wow, another overwhelming thing to throw on the fire. Arianna was sleeping peacefully in her crib. She really was the most beautiful baby in the world, so tiny, peaceful, and perfect.

"Here she is." I took his hand. "Arianna Rayne Sandoval. Your daughter."

Chapter 19

Sinclair

She was an amazingly beautiful little being. I couldn't do anything but stare at her perfect fingers and toes. Her tiny face was angelic. Everything about the child was divine. I could see why Reyna wanted to rush back home to her. I'm surprised I even got her for one night. It hurt that she'd given Arianna her last name, but whose name would she have given her? She didn't know who I was. In any other context, I'd be so grateful and relieved she wasn't saddled with me or my legacy. Looking at her now, I wanted nothing more than to legally claim her as mine.

I decided not to broach the subject with Reyna at that moment, she was right, she was processing a lot, as was I. I made a note to address it at some later date. I wanted them both to have my name. As I stood before that crib in an old Hollywood apartment with her delightful roommates, it felt like family. The only person missing was my brother Sage… Shelton, we could abandon somewhere, but Sage would love it here.

He'd especially love Melody. I noted her playing the guitar, and she was quite good. I couldn't even count how many times I'd walked in and caught Sage playing the guitar, just as she was. This all felt so right. I wanted to reach down and scoop little Arianna into my arms, but I'd heard rumors about how hard babies were to get to sleep, so I left her to rest.

"She's perfect, like a miniature you," I said as I wrapped my arms around Reyna and kissed her. "She's perfect, Rey. I'm in awe."

"Yeah, she's amazing." Reyna's face cast an ethereal light.

I'd seen her have that look before, momentarily while we were having sex. Such an indescribable beauty. I couldn't pinpoint it, but now looking at her gazing at our daughter, I knew exactly what that look was... it was love, pure and unconditional love.

"Thank you for allowing me into her life, Reyna. I promise I will do everything in my power to honor my role as her father. We don't have to do this now, but this week, I want you and me to discuss finances and her care." As I expected, she moved to protest, but I put my finger up to her lips.

"No, you'll not fight me on this one. I'm her father. If you want, we can get a paternity test to prove it, but I'm one hundred percent sure it's not necessary." Even though there may have been a remote chance, the baby wasn't mine, I didn't care. I believed Reyna. And if for some reason, I was wrong, I was still going to be this child's father... forever.

"She's yours; there hasn't been anyone else." I moved past the disappointed look on Reyna's face, most likely motivated by my even mentioning paternity.

"I have absolutely no doubt, and I'll make sure she's well cared for." I felt compelled to kiss Reyna, so I leaned in and seized her mouth.

We kissed passionately for a moment before I broke away. If I continued to kiss her, I'd have to make love to her... truly and earnestly make love.

What we'd been doing was fun, but I wanted to love her... give myself over and never look back. Instead, I left her to her roommates and our baby.

"I know you want some time love, so I'm going to go. Monday, though, at some point, I'd like to figure out when we'll see each other again." I took her hand and kissed her knuckles, wanting oh so much more.

"Okay. Let's figure it out on Monday." She seemed a bit dazed, but I accepted it as being just too much, as she had said.

She walked me to the door. Her roommates were still there. One was on her laptop, the other on the guitar. I waved to them casually, "Bye everyone. I hope to see you soon." I kissed Reyna again. "I'll see you on Monday. Be at work on time," I pretended to be the tyrant as I slapped her ass, and I walked away only turning to say, "Goodbye, sweetheart."

"Bye, Sin." She closed the door behind me.

I'd never felt so alone as I did standing in the hallway of her apartment building. I was close to her, to them… and yet so far away.

It seemed like I'd left a piece of my heart behind. I'd only known Reyna for a short time, but she was such an incredible human and our baby… all I wanted to do was hold her and be her father. I was lulling myself into the fantasy that raising a child was easy and a commitment to a woman I barely knew wasn't hard. My heart, though, was tugging at me, telling me to march back into her apartment, scoop her up, and bring my family home. God knows I had enough room for them… all of them, even the roommates.

Life, with all its privileges, suddenly seemed so unfair. All I wanted was to hang out with my baby, Reyna, and her lovely roommates. Instead, I was in my Land Rover heading back to the mansion on the hill… the loneliest place on earth. These huge emotions I couldn't place. The only thing that could give me solace was my passion for movies. So, I spent the rest of Saturday watching an independent movie marathon in my basement movie theater. Michael brought me lunch and dinner there and probably worried a little about my state of mind. He didn't say anything other than a mention in passing that the woman I had over the night before was lovely. I couldn't have agreed with him more.

Monday was equally torturous, if not more so. I got into the office early after spending a good deal of time laboring over what I was going to wear. I felt giddy delight knowing I'd see Reyna again, and I wanted to wear something both masculine and sexy. No one was in the office when I got there, but I'd played out the moment of her arrival over and over again in my head.

In truth, all I wanted to do was lock her in my office and make love to her on the sofa, but she deserved better. She wasn't the kind of person you bent over a table. I was realizing this, and while our sex was fun, I needed to make love.

Unfortunately, I was going to have to pretend nothing was happening between us at work. It was in neither of our best interests to announce our relationship as we didn't really have one… yet. I had planned to let people know soon. It was my company, and I didn't want to hide my child or my interest in Reyna; however, it would mean finding her another job, and we weren't ready for that step… at least I wasn't.

I knew the moment she arrived. People had begun filing in, and I heard their conversations outside my door. It was the usual morning banter, but every word set my nerves on edge. Why wouldn't she just get there already? Then, after what seemed like hours, I heard the sweet trill of her melodic voice. Not only that but suddenly the air was filled with the faint scent of sandalwood and lavender. She gave everyone a kind greeting as she made her way to her cubical outside of my office.

Finally, she'd arrived. Perfectly on time, she was as calm and effervescent as ever. I was the one on edge. Every moment waiting for her was torture.

She waved at me as she set her things down and sat at her desk. "Good morning, Mr. Harris," she said with a smile.

"Reyna," I barked in a curt tone of voice. She knew I hated being called Mr. Harris. She was being snarky and was going to get away with it, because to most, I was Mr. Harris.

I smiled, hiding my agitation. "Good morning, Reyna. Mr. Harris is a math teacher, and I'm your boss. Could you come in here for a moment please?" I sounded more stern than I'd hoped as a look of concern flashed across her face.

"Sure." She casually sauntered into my office, holding her notepad.

As soon as she walked in, I closed the door and turned her toward me. "Good morning, Mr. Harris?" I couldn't help myself; I grabbed her and kissed with all my pent-up emotions.

My tongue demanded entry into her mouth as I tasted her minty-fresh breath and pressed my demanding cock against her mini skirt. "I missed you," I breathed as I finally parted from her lips.

"I guess you did." She laughed.

Her hand came up to my mouth and smoothed over my swollen lips. I bit it as she traced my mouth and sucked on it. She pulled her thumb from me and gave me a playfully pained look.

"Ouch, you little monster." She crossed her eyes and shook her head. "You know, Electric Plum isn't your color." She smoothed the rest of her lipstick off of my mouth. "You're going to get us into a lot of trouble, Mr. Harris if you don't behave… remember the indelible wisdom etched upon your happy trail. Let's not get me fired, shall we? Now was there any real business you needed to discuss?"

Ah... how was I going to get through the day without having her? "No, carry on." I slapped her ass and turned back to my desk.

She glared at me, then opened the door, and returned to her cube.

Ken, the asshole was there, ready to pounce. "So, how was your weekend?" he asked planted against her cubical wall.

He was an incredibly handsome young man and was going places in the company if I didn't fire him for looking at Reyna first. Molly loved him, and admittedly, he was a hard worker, good at development. He'd already brought us one amazing script we were able to snag before a bidding war began, and he was working on securing another. He was sort of indispensable. I, however, was brewing an intense hatred for the man.

"I just did weekend things. You?" Reyna fired up her computer and nearly ignored him.

I wanted to rush over to Ken and scratch his eyes out but refrained.

"Well, we had the premiere on Friday. Can you believe our opening weekend? We rivaled Predator, the Regency Pictures flick. I think we either beat them or tied for biggest box office. We're on fire..."

"No, Ken, you imbecile," I wanted to say. *I'm* on fire. It's my company, and at the moment, he was on my land... oh if only murder were legal.

"I was pretty shattered after the party. I didn't really see you there. I mean you were only there like for a minute. I looked everywhere for you. One minute you were with Sinclair and the next you were completely gone. What was that all about?" He leaned in closer, trying to get her attention.

I was going to kill him. Ken was better suited for Reyna. He was more her age. She was twenty-eight, and I had just turned thirty-nine in July. They had much more in common than she and I did. He was young and up and coming, and so was she. I, on the other hand, was a demanding millionaire who was used to getting what he wanted. The only thing Reyna and I really had in common was our baby, but at least we had her. There was other stuff too, but we were still working our way into each other's lives… so fuck him.

"My car broke down," she answered plainly, "and I needed to get it to the shop before it closed. Sinclair knew about it, and since my boss isn't a total tool, he left the party to give me a ride home from the shop," she tossed off casually.

"How gallant. So, that's what happened. I'd heard you went home with him," he lowered his voice to a whisper, so I could barely hear what he was saying.

"God, no." She laughed. I thought her response was a bit excessive. "I ordered a pizza, and my roommates and I binged-watched Stranger Things on Netflix. Not very gossip-worthy, I'm afraid." She shrugged her shoulders and attempted to go back to work.

"Guess not. I slept in on Saturday; then we did some pickup shots for the rest of the weekend. I'm producing this cool indie film. You should meet the director; I bet he'd have a small part for you. We still have a few roles left to fill."

No… oh no. She is not going to be in that fucker's movie.

"Sorry, I'm an abysmal actor." She wasn't an abysmal actor at all actually. She was quite good at role-playing, but it worked. I didn't want her going anywhere near him.

"You're so gorgeous, though…" He was going to be a dead man soon.

"Thanks, but I'm definitely not gorgeous enough to make up for a shocking lack of skill." She flashed him a smile and turned her back on him to pick up a pile of scripts.

"I'll respectfully disagree. You should see the first film we did; it's on YouTube." He hovered over her and opened the web browser on her computer.

That was enough; I couldn't stand it anymore. I cleared my throat to get their attention. "No personal web browsing on the company computer," I yelled out my office door.

"Oh shit, sorry I forgot, Sinclair." He sheepishly exited out of the browser and meandered back to his cube, which was just a few short paces from hers. "Guess I better start work." He gave me a shit-eating grin, and I wasn't amused.

"Why don't you do that," I almost growled.

I could tell it was hard for Reyna to keep a straight face. Somehow I felt like I was the butt of a joke. It was uncomfortable.

"Are you free for lunch today?" he whisper-yelled from his cube.

"No," I answered for her. "She's working with me at lunch today," I said sternly letting him know I could still hear his conversation.

He disregarded me, "What about cocktails after work?" The fucking nerve of that man.

"She's staying late," I answered again.

"Hey Sin, way to honor your work/life policy. The poor lady needs food and drink, just like the rest of us." He had the nerve to talk back to me.

"It's only a couple of days; she'll live," I dismissed as Reyna took a call for me and my fun, terrorizing the stupid male homing in on my girl was over.

"It's Don Richards on line one," she cooed sweetly ending my cockfight with Ken.

Chapter 20

Reyna

It was funny to see Sinclair so jealous of Ken. I was highly amused. Being at work with him was harder than I thought it would be. I was so excited to see him; it was almost like Christmas morning when I was a little kid. I made sure to come into work exactly on time so as not to appear too eager, and then he pulled me into his office, and we kissed. From that moment forward, I could barely concentrate on anything other than Sinclair.

I wish Ken knew how annoying he was. Even if Sinclair and I weren't dating, I still wouldn't have gone out with him. The pissing war between Ken and Sinclair was going to be the end of me. I couldn't balance both hotheads, so I just focused on my work and tried to ignore them. In Sinclair's case, unfortunately, that was impossible.

When he was done with his phone call, he asked me to come into his office again. Even though I wanted him to kiss me, I sort of didn't want it. I was afraid he might try more than a kiss, and there was no way I was going for that. Even if I were married to the guy, I wouldn't be fucking him in the office. It wasn't something I could do. No offense to those who could, hats off to them, but having sex at my place of work, especially with my boss, was not gonna happen. Ever.

I walked in ready to face whatever he had in store for me.

I closed the door behind me and just blurted out, "Sinclair, there is no way I am going to have sex with you in the office." I shot him a fierce stare.

He laughed. "Ha, you read my mind, but you're right. I wouldn't dream of having sex with you here. I don't have much time. Since the film blew up this weekend, we're on everyone's call list. I have meetings all day. I won't have much time to talk with you today. We do have a working lunch, but I'm the only one working. You can use my office if you'd like to eat and pump and just have some time if you need it." Ah… he was being him again, sweet, loving—this was the Sinclair I liked.

"Are you sure? I have to admit, pumping in the bathroom is pretty gross." I screwed my face to make a point.

"I know there's no place for you to pump except for the bathroom. It's clean, but how awful you have to sit on a toilet. I'm working with HR to ratify this issue, but I need your permission to tell them you have a baby. I'm hoping to turn one of the storerooms into a comfortable space for lactating mothers. It's not just for you; Alejandra in marketing is pregnant and would also appreciate it." Wow, he'd given this a lot of thought.

"Sounds perfect." I smiled and gave him a quick kiss on the cheek. "Thanks."

"No need for thanks, we should have done it a long time ago," he said as he went back to his work. "I'll try and catch up with you tonight."

"Okay." I went back to my desk, still wanting to spend more time with him.

He had meetings all day and didn't return until everyone was starting to go home that night. I knew I'd have to leave and pick up Arianna from Mrs. Effleman, but I waited for him so I could at least say goodbye for the day.

When he finally returned, it was an hour after most people had already gone home. Ken, of course, was still there as was his boss, who returned from the same meeting with Sinclair.

"Ah, you two are still chained to your desks I see," Ken's

boss mentioned as she walked up to us.

"It's cool. Reyna's been keeping me company," Ken interjected with a charming smile.

It was, of course, a lie. I wasn't keeping him company. I was working and trying my best to ignore him.

"Yep, I'm sitting here working. Ooooh, such good company," I mocked sarcastically.

Sinclair looked positively evil until he heard me pronounce my innocence.

"Well, you two should shut it down. We need to go home. Work/life balance, people." Sinclair looked directly at Ken when he said it.

"I'm done." I logged off and closed my laptop. "Just waiting for the boss to unchain me." I gave Sinclair a seductive wink, and his eyes flared open.

"Wait a sec, and I'll walk you to your car." I wasn't sure he meant to say that in front of everyone, but he said it.

"I can go with her," Ken chimed in. "I parked right next to her." If you could have seen the rage Sinclair was holding back. I found it truly comical.

Ken's boss said, "Since when has the car park become so dangerous? Maybe we should all go down together. Bring our machetes and such." She shook her head as she walked into her office, leaving the three of us feeling awkward.

"I just need to grab my bag," Sinclair announced.

It took him only a minute before he was ready to walk out. Ken was scrambling to get himself ready when Molly called out from her office.

"Ken, before you go, can you help me with one thing."
And that was it. Molly killed it for him. Sinclair almost burst into
laughter. Ken flashed us a smug smile, and we left.

"See ya tomorrow," I threw out as we were leaving.

As soon as we were in the elevator, Sinclair grabbed me,
and we kissed. We tongue fought each other for the duration of
the ride, and when the doors opened, he made his move.

"Can I convince you to come home with me tonight?" he
asked, looking like a forlorn little boy.

"I'm already really late picking up the baby." I tried to say
it as kindly as I could, sympathetic to his plea. I wanted to be with
him too, but I couldn't see it happening tonight. I couldn't leave
the baby again so soon.

"I understand." He was noticeably disappointed but had to
know I was making the right choice. "I guess I'll see you
tomorrow then."

Poor guy, you could have wiped his face off the floor he
was so sad.

"What about you and I getting together this weekend?" I
tried to cheer him up.

"What? No, I can't wait that long." His face morphed into
an impatient and angry sort of expression.

"I'll be seeing you at work. Certainly, you can go a week
without the bump and grind." I wasn't sure he could, but he'd
have to.

"No, I can't pretend to be your boss and not the man who
is falling head over heels for you. It's torture." He took a deep
breath. "Wednesday? Bring the baby to my place after work, and

I'll have Salvatore make us dinner. Then, you and I can chill." It was weird having him try to sound like a Millennial.

"Unless you've changed completely in two days, I don't think we'll be doing much 'chillin'.' Sounds fun, though. Let's plan for Wednesday. You sure you want me to bring Arianna?" It would be an absolute dream if I could, but I didn't want him saying things just to entice me.

"Absolutely!" By the look on his face, I knew he meant it.

Surprisingly, after the brief conversation, he let me go home. He was rather pitiful just standing there as I drove off. I felt for the guy because if it were me, I'd be standing there too.

He texted me the whole way home… and throughout the night. If we could barely spend one night apart, how were we ever going to survive working together every day pretending we didn't care about each other?

The next day I was excited to see Sinclair but tired. He'd texted me all night long, way past my usual bedtime. He told me stories, gave me play by plays on what he was doing at exact moments in the evening and talking dirty about ways he wanted to excite my body.

I couldn't deny he made me hot. I actually masturbated for the first time in forever, thinking about the things he suggested we do on Wednesday. When I came into work, I saw him sitting in his office and felt an overwhelming sense of peace being in his presence again. I was falling hard. The more time we spent apart, the more I wanted to be near him. It was strange. The first few weeks we worked together, I wasn't allowing myself to feel anything. I hadn't met the man hiding deep within, and I just pretended it wasn't him, the dark angel who changed my life.

We nearly rushed into each other's arms when we saw each

other that next morning. Luckily we didn't. News had just hit the press and was all over the internet. Of course, it was Ken who announced this juicy bit of gossip as soon as we came in. He was reading from the Variety website. Christopher Regent had been indicted on sexual-harassment charges by a former assistant.

"Hey, didn't you work for him?" Ken asked, his eyes piercing.

I could hardly breathe. "Yes," I whispered.

"According to this article, he did some very fucked up stuff." Ken sounded almost disbelieving.

Every single nerve in my body froze. I was not the person who launched the lawsuit against Chris, but just the mention of his name and the lewd acts he'd committed against this woman were enough to paralyze me. I remembered every horrible thing he did. Things I'd never mentioned to anyone, but kept bottled up inside, still haunted me almost every single lewd act mentioned in the article had also been done to me. Ken read about the invitations to dinner that became forced fellatio. He also mentioned how Chris threatened a person's job if they didn't attend an event as his date. He was accused of sexual harassment and misconduct as well as three counts of rape.

While I never allowed him to get too far, dinner conversations were always sexually inappropriate. I'd usually have to shove him off of me to escape untouched. The things he did get away with, that I couldn't easily fend off, were times when he copped a feel of my ass, pussy, or breasts. I'd pinch the skin just under his arm, near his armpit to get him off me.

He'd laugh and pretend it was some immature joke. "Boys locker room stuff," he used to say. When his finger pressed hard into my vagina after a notes meeting, I took to wearing lined wool slacks. Even in the summer, I wore them to avoid him ever getting into close contact with that sensitive region of my body ever again. Despite everything I did to thwart him, the constant nagging and pressuring was relentless.

By the time Ken had finished reading the article, tears were welling in my eyes. I had to sit down to stabilize my shaky insides. I knew Chris had raped women. He talked about sex all the time. He always alluded to the acts being consensual. Because he was such a maverick in the bedroom, women flocked to him, he'd say. I nearly choked when I heard that the first time.

He was obsessed with sex and told about countless encounters which seemed more like rape to me than unbridled passion. He also used to boast about how many bastards he had out there he wasn't paying for. The slutty bitches spread their legs so easily for him, why should he have to pay for their promiscuity?

Remembering all of it sent me into a scared and fearful place. I hadn't realized how bad it all was. Being away from Chris and having time to heal helped me understand that what I dealt with day after day was sexual harassment and abuse. I literally went into battle every day to save my integrity and emotional well-being.

As soon as Ken stopped reading, his voice was snide and judgmental. "Everyone in Hollywood knows what an asshole Christopher was. If anyone was stupid enough to take a job with him, they should pretty much have known they'd be 'spreadin' their legs.'" What the hell?

"Are you making light of this?" I couldn't believe how insensitive he was.

"No offense, Reyna. Rumor has it you kicked the douche's ass." He gave me a fake smile.

"I was fired because my bathroom breaks were too

long… but it was hell." I looked at him dead on.

Rape and sexual misconduct were absolutely no joking matter. I saw the look in Sinclair's eyes. He was barely holding his temper. I hadn't realized he was staring at me, but the compassion in his gaze melted my heart. We never spoke about my time with Chris. He saw us on Halloween and saw Chris briefly at the premiere. Sinclair really didn't know how much I had to endure with Chris, but I think he understood without knowing the details.

Chapter 21

Sinclair

"The article asks for women who have witnessed or been a victim of Christopher Regent's actions to come forward." Ken gave Reyna a cocky glare. "They have an email address and a phone number where people can get in touch with them. Maybe you should call, Reyna."

Reyna looked pale. "I'm sure there are plenty of people who have experienced far worse," she dismissed.

"I hope more women come forward because that man needs to go to jail for the rest of his life for what he's done," I said, making my opinion clear.

After that uncomfortable start to our day, we moved on. When the dailies were delivered an hour later, I asked Reyna to join me in the office to watch them and take notes. She seemed more like herself when she bounded into my office.

"I missed you," she whispered as she closed the door behind her.

"I've been crazy without you," I countered scooping her into my arms. "I don't think I can last until tomorrow night. Is there any way I can get you tonight, tomorrow, and maybe every night after?" I was trying not to sound desperate, but I was.

She laughed, keeping the mood light. "Um… I do have a life, but I don't think I can wait until tomorrow either."

"I've been giving this some thought," I started, "and I've spoken with Lorna, my housekeeper. She wouldn't mind watching Arianna while you are at the house. There's not much for her to do there. I think she's dying for something meaningful to set her mind to. She would love to watch the baby." I was so nervous, hoping Reyna would say, yes, I could hardly think of anything else. "Tonight when we leave, you can go get the baby and stuff for another 'slumber party,' and I'll meet you at the house." I was tingling with excitement.

The idea of having Reyna and the baby home with me was thrilling. She stared at me, and for a moment I thought she might not agree, but much to my great relief, she accepted my offer. Thank God. It was nearly impossible to get through the rest of the day. Daydreaming about making love to her all night long was what kept me going.

We said our goodbyes at the end of the day, and I almost rushed out behind her; however, with eyes all over the place, I held myself back. She texted me when she got to the house and said she and Arianna were with Lorna and Michael. I walked in and inadvertently overheard a conversation that wasn't intended for my ears.

"It's going to be so nice to have this little one around," I heard Lorna say. "This place is so big and lonely at times. Sinclair is a quiet man. He has lots of friends, but he doesn't often have them over. I actually think he's quite lonely. His brother Sage is the outgoing one, and none of us really see much of Shelton. She's so beautiful and perfect."

Lorna blushed as I walked in. She was holding the baby, and Reyna's face lit up the moment she saw me. "I hope I'm not interrupting. I got a phone call just as I was leaving the office. Our lead actor for The Morning Star film was having issues. I had to talk him out of the tree, but I'm here now."

I walked over to Lorna and outstretched my arms. "Can I hold her?" I looked at Reyna for approval.

"Of course," she said as Lorna gave me the baby.

"She's heaven, Sinclair," Lorna said with adoration in her eyes.

Nerves gripped me as I held Arianna's tiny body. She was so little and delicate. As soon as she was cradled into my embrace, she looked up at me with her big beautiful green eyes, my eyes. I melted. I was her father, and I'd love and protect her for the rest of my life. I kissed her sweet head. It smelled like baby powder and innocence.

"She's everything," I sighed.

Reyna walked to my side and stroked Arianna's wisps of brown hair over her soft head. I think the baby regarded me with the same overwhelming wonder I had for her. I could have sat and held her all night, but I was starving, and I figured Reyna must be too.

"Salvatore made some delicious vegetarian Greek dishes for you to try. I'll watch the baby," Lorna announced, opening her arms eager to take the baby back.

"Do you want to feed her or anything?" I asked before releasing the child to her, unsure of whether we'd see her again, given Lorna's eagerness.

"Maybe I should," Reyna laughed as two grown adults fawned and cooed over Arianna.

She took the baby from me and held her to her breast, giving her a nipple. The baby immediately started to feed. She looked perfect in Reyna's arms. I could see why the Madonna and child became such an iconic image; there was nothing more beautiful than a mother and baby.

"Here," I offered, leading her into the living room. "Why

don't you feed her in here, on the couch."

"Thanks." She settled into the seat as I heard Arianna make sweet suckling sounds. All I could do was stare in awe of them. I read an article about fathers supporting breastfeeding mothers. The article explained how male partners could take care of the mother as they nurtured their child. It talked about things like foot rubs, back rubs, getting the mom water or snacks.

"I'll get you something to drink. Do you want juice, mineral water, tea?" I knew she probably didn't want wine while feeding Arianna, but I hoped she would later.

"Some chamomile tea would be nice." She looked up at me, serene and happy.

"Right away." I ran off to get the tea.

I made the tea myself; I wanted to serve her. When I returned with it, Arianna was fast asleep on Reyna's nipple. A warm feeling overtook me, and all I wanted to do was scoop the both of them into my arms. Instead, I set the tea next to Reyna and asked if I could take our sleeping baby from her so she could join me for dinner.

Reyna had brought a pack-n-play. I set it up in the guest room right next to my bedroom so we could hear her if she woke up at night. I put her down in the little pack-n-play and was happy she didn't wake up screaming and yelling. I expected she would at some point, but luckily for me it wasn't that night. I came back into the living room a complete success.

We had an excellent meal together, and I learned more about Arianna's routine and schedule. She goes down at about eight o'clock but would be up again at midnight.

"We better eat and get busy fast before part one of the

evening is over." I was seriously planning this out.

"Maybe we should," she agreed, looking hot and seductive.

"Now… how about now?" I asked as I stood, having eaten enough.

"Now, is good." She smiled as I scooped her into my arms and carried her to my bedroom. I tiptoed past the guest room and laid Reyna on the bed.

"So, I've had a few nights to contemplate how I'll ravage you, and I've decided that tonight, at least part one of tonight, is all about you. I want to love every inch of your body. I will make love to you so well you'll never be able to think of any other man ever!" My voice slid into a seductive command.

She laid back and spread her legs gently. "I'm all yours."

I jumped onto the bed and helped her take her dress off, exposing her gorgeous lace panties. "I like these," I commented on the lingerie. "Are they new?"

She cocked her pretty head. "I guess Victoria doesn't have a secret anymore." She laid down and spread her legs wider, beckoning me to do what I would with her.

I slid the panties off and started feasting. I kissed her inner thighs as she giggled, my stubble tickling her sensitive skin as she tried to wiggle away. I continued to the tuft of hair framing her pussy, smelling the clean curls. She was sweet and sensuous; I loved eating her pussy. I circled my tongue around her love button as the familiar rut of her hips responded to my attention.

I slid my tongue into her vagina and enjoyed the feeling of her bucking into my thrusts. I knew what to do to make her climax and also knew she needed a few orgasms before she could be comfortably penetrated. Her fingers knotted in my hair as she arched up to my invading mouth. The sound of her high pitched mewl as she shuddered her release was delightful. Seeing her face in the throes of ecstasy made me love her more.

As she came down from her high, I snaked up her body, fully clothed, my cock begging for freedom, but this first course was all about love... all about the mother of my child.

"You are so good at that." She sighed, floating down from the heavens.

"I'm good at other things too," I purred as I dipped my head into her neck and bit the soft skin.

"What the..." She wiggled then stilled, her skin lodged in my mouth. "Are you biting me?" she asked in disbelief. "So... the rumors are true, you're a vampire." She laughed and slid her hand into my pants grabbing my underwear-clad cock.

"Hey, this is supposed to be about you..." I scoffed, feeling her tug on my dick.

"Yep, and I want you," she whispered, "I've freaking waited two whole days for this.

"Right." I obeyed and undid my pants, chuffed them off while she unbuttoned my shirt with a renewed fervor.

As soon as I was naked, and we'd finished undressing her, I worshiped her breasts. Having just fed the baby, they were raw and sensitive. I kissed each nipple and lovingly smoothed my tongue around the red skin. Her arms clasped around my body and drew me closer moaning sweetly in my ear. After I lavished each breast with love and attention, my cock planted between us. Feeling the warmth of her skin on me, I captured her mouth and kissed her with all the love in my heart.

I wanted her to know we were equals, sexually and

emotionally.

"I may be your boss at times, Reyna, but know I see you as my equal," I said as I gathered her into my lap, holding her body tightly to mine.

"Good," she responded, wiggling herself onto my very extremely erect cock.

She easily guided me into her and slowly stroked her vagina up and down on me, her tight pussy suctioning my dick like a dream. Instinctively my arms held her, and I positioned our bodies so I was able to jettison in and out faster. Holding her close, the friction between us built. The lower half of my body did as it pleased, pulsing and pumping until the humming call to cum beckoned. Her head cradled into the nape of my neck as she surrendered to my impassioned thrusting. Her delicate arms seized my back, fingernails raking my skin as she came hard on my cock. Since I'd been away from her for so long, I found my release moments later. We collapsed on the bed together, and I shuffled her into my arms.

"I'm addicted to you," I said, trying to catch my breath. "I want you and Arianna to move in. Let's do this crazy thing. We have plenty of room. I can't do this again, going two days without was torture. Don't say no," I commanded.

She responded by hitting me with a pillow. "Snap out of it!" Her reaction threw me off, and I laughed, hard. She's right; what was I doing? "I'm not moving in with you, that would be insane. We work together and live together after dating for what? Two days?" Her harsh jest made me laugh.

People were a little afraid of me at times, but she had never been. She never feared my retaliation, and she loved to play. I hit her back with the pillow, softly. "I can still ask, can't I?"

She smiled. "Sure. You can always ask."

Just as the two of us were having a post-coital snicker, Arianna's tiny cry came as a distant call from the other room. It was sweet and demure at first, but boy did it escalate until it was a rather unbearable wail.

"Wow, who knew such a little thing could make so much noise." I was shocked.

"And cue reality in… five, four, three, two…" Reyna slipped out of bed, grabbed her shirt and her underwear from the floor, and walked out the door.

Chapter 22

Reyna

I knew Arianna was bound to wake up. Usually, she'd wait till midnight, but she'd gotten up at ten before; it was becoming a bit of a habit. She wasn't hungry but needed a diaper change. She had quite a messy diaper, the kind that really made your stomach turn. I was grumbling under my breath when Sinclair walked in, shirtless, only wearing his pajama pants.

"Diaper change?" he asked, sounding curious as he peered over my shoulder. "Wow, yuck. Who would believe a little thing like that could make such a mess. She's a little badass, just like her mother." he said, slapping my ass. "Move over." He scooted me to the side and took my place. "Okay." He'd lost a little of his momentum facing her poo covered diaper and baby butt. "So, what am I doing here?"

"I can do it." I chuckled at his enthusiasm, ready to replace him.

"Nope, I got this." He grabbed the wipes and a diaper, armed and ready.

"Okay." I figured if he was honest about us being here, he was going to have to do diaper changes, midnight feedings, and the works. "Gently lift her legs up and wipe from the front to the back with the wipes. Make sure you get all of the poop off and she's really clean before you put on a new diaper."

Watching him struggle with the poop was funny, but he did a fairly good job of it. Arianna seemed quite amused by his effort. Other than putting the diaper on loose and crooked, he did a fine job. When he went to the bathroom to wash his hands, I put her diaper on better and cradled her in my arms. Usually, she'd go right back to sleep after I dimmed the lights and sang a lullaby, so that's what I did. Sinclair came back in as I was singing to her, and she was drifting off in my arms.

As I swayed with her lulling her to sleep again, Sinclair came up behind me and swayed with me, humming with my tune. It was a wonderful feeling having him this involved with me and the baby. I'd never thought I'd have this. Even if it was a fleeting moment, it was perfect. After a few songs, Arianna fell asleep, and I was able to place her back in the pack-n-play.

"Thanks for your help."

"I'm going to be a bigger part of this," he vowed as he moved a strand of wayward hair from my face and kissed my temple. "So, are you game for a movie before bed?"

"Sure, that sounds fun." A little diversion from the intensity of all of "this" was very tempting.

"I usually host a private movie screening before I hit the sheets." He laughed as he escorted me out of the guest room. "I'll text Lorna and tell her to stay around and keep her ears out for the baby."

"Isn't she off work by now?' I didn't want to be an imposition.

"Trust me, she doesn't mind," he said, texting.

We walked through the halls and down two flights of stairs to an underground movie theater with about thirty real movie theater seats. He turned on the lights, and his face had a childish glow.

"So what do you want to see? he asked as he fired up the 25-foot movie screen. He had thousands of movies to pick from.

The screen was filled from top to bottom with tiny movie posters to choose from.

"Oh my God, I could spend the whole night choosing. How do you even pick?" I asked, seriously overwhelmed.

"Well, I kind of have these movie marathons, like a private movie festival. At the moment, I'm having a slasher, gorefest." His face reddened as he pressed a button on the remote and the screen changed to horrific-looking horror movies. "It was the only thing that would keep my mind off of you."

"Wow, well, um… yikes. I'm not usually one for a slasher, because they give me nightmares, but since I've got a bed buddy tonight, let's go for it." I was terrified, but also a little exhilarated; it would be fun, holding on to him through all the jumpy parts.

"Ah, this will be fun." He stroked my arm and pressed a button on the remote. The screen came to life, dark, eerie, and menacing.

"I'm sure I'm going to regret this." I cuddled into his arm, my stomach already in knots.

"I know I'm not." He tightened his arm around me.

Sure enough, the movie was horrible… truly violent, disgusting, and scary. He laughed at the gruesome parts, and I closed my eyes. It was fun like we were teenagers on a date. As much as I hated the movie, I loved being with him. He had a dark side, but it was safe and boyish… I loved discovering yet another facet of his personality. When the movie was over, my body was tense and terrified.

"That movie was so fucked up," I said rolling my neck, trying to release the stress.

"You okay?" He was earnestly concerned.

"Just a little shaken up." I gave him a tentative smile. "Did they really play that movie in the theaters?"

"Little confession." His smile was devilish and childish. "It's a film we're thinking of acquiring; it hasn't been released yet."

"Maybe you shouldn't let that one out of the box." My face screwed into a grimace.

"It could use a little editing, but it would be a hit on the horror circuit. I had no idea, and I seriously mean this, you were such a wuss." He laughed as he massaged my knotted shoulders. "I thought you had a Gothic script. I just figured you were good with horror."

"It's a romance." I rolled my eyes. "I like sexy vampires and fallen angels, you know, like the one I had a baby with." I glared at him, teasing.

"Oops," he smirked. "You wanna watch something else to make up for it?"

"Isn't it midnight?" I was feeling really sleepy, and knowing Arianna might be up again soon, I thought bed might be a good next item on our agenda.

"It's one in the morning. We should probably get to bed; it's a work night. I'm a bit of a night owl, I lose track sometimes." He did seem very perky despite the late hour.

He took me back to his room. I checked in on Arianna who was, thankfully, still sleeping. I was surprised to see Lorna there with her but grateful there was someone watching over her while Sinclair and I endured that movie.

"How was the screening?" she asked quietly, making sure not to wake the baby.

"Scary, he really has some psycho killer tendencies doesn't he?" I widened my eyes.

"Oh sweetie, we never let him rope us into going down there with him. He watches some very weird stuff." She was being serious and had a sweet mature woman's concern; it was motherly and kind.

"You're telling me." I stared at Arianna for a moment, just marveling at her sweetness, sleeping there so peacefully.

"Goodnight, I'll see you both in the morning," Lorna said then turned to walk out.

"Thank you so much for looking after her."

"My pleasure."

When I returned to Sinclair's room, he was undressed and in bed already. He drew back the covers, offering me to join him. I scooted in and turned out the light.

"Quickie before bed?" he asked as he lifted my leg over his hardness.

"You sure have the sex drive of a vampire," I commented, spreading my legs for him. "If you sprout fangs and rip out my throat like what happened to the girl in the movie, I'm leaving and never coming back."

He chuckled as he slipped my panties off and used his fingers to prepare me. It didn't take long to make me wet. Our lovemaking was slow and sensual. We made love laying side by side, looking into each other's eyes. His cock softly pulsed in and out in a sensual rhythm, never breaking the pace. Even when we both reached our climax together, it was almost balletic. I drifted off to sleep in his arms, sated and filled with his love.

I hadn't even heard Arianna get up later that night. I noticed the sudden coldness and felt his absence. I must have been sleeping much harder than I usually slept because when I looked around the room, he was gone. My phone said it was almost three in the morning, but he wasn't anywhere to be found. I was still wearing my shirt, but no panties as I rushed to the guest room to check on Arianna.

Sinclair was sprawled out on the couch with Arianna sleeping safely in his embrace. She must have woken up in the middle of the night. I was surprised I missed it but loved seeing the two that way. I quietly closed the door and returned to his bed. I waited for him there for a while, but he never came back.

The next morning, a blaring alarm bolted me out of bed. Sinclair still wasn't beside me. I figured he was still sleeping with the baby, so I went in to wake them. I found him changing her diaper.

"Hey Momma, bring those boobs over here. I'm pretty sure she's hungry," he commanded as he finished the last of the diaper change and handed her over. "I'll make breakfast." He was happier than I'd ever seen him.

"I can't believe you slept with her on the couch; you must be exhausted." I really was shocked.

"I'm good. She's amazing, but we'd better hurry if we're going to have enough time to eat, shower, drop her off, and get to work on time. When you're done feeding her, there's a guest bathroom, right over there." He pointed to the door next to the closet. "And I'll meet you in the kitchen. We'll leave in forty-five minutes." He was very efficient, back to being the boss again.

Despite the efficiency and curt commands, I loved him. He was really making space in his life for us, and I appreciated the effort and the sleep. I hadn't had a full night of sleep in ages. Even when I was here last, we played all night long, so it wasn't very restful. Unbelievably, we made it out the door on time and got Arianna to Ms. Effleman without missing a beat. She was happy to meet Sinclair and gave him the same adoring look most women did when they first saw him.

All was going great until on the ride into work he mentioned Chris and the lawsuit being mounted against him.

"I know you don't want to talk about this," he started, seeing the angered look on my face.

"He didn't rape me, Sinclair, he was just a fucking, horrible asshole… daily." I fumed.

"Right. Every day you had to ward off his sexual advances. I saw what he did to you on Halloween. If that's what he felt comfortable doing in public, I can only imagine what he must've tried in private. I'm glad you got away from him, but there are others who aren't so lucky. Truthfully, we probably owe him a thank you note for putting us together. It was first your beauty, then my need to rescue you that brought us together that night. I think you should do this, not only for you but for the other poor women who have the misfortune of working for him." He was so serious; I knew he wouldn't give me a chance to wiggle away from this.

I took a deep breath. "He just… it was just touching. He only tried to kiss me once… Oh, and he wanted me to touch his junk." As I tried to rationalize the sexual harassment away, I began to remember. "Words… stories, innuendos…" The more I said, the more I saw the truth.

"Propositions, threats…" he interrupted.

"But if I go through with this, it'll bring a spotlight down on me, and people will find out about the baby and us… it's going to get really messy, Sinclair." I didn't want him dragged into this.

"I don't care. I want you to contact the prosecutor. I'll stand by you. I'm not worried about myself. I don't abuse women, and I never have." He was so confident and committed; I couldn't do anything but accept.

"Okay." I nearly whispered, "I'll call when we get to work."

"Great, okay, elephant one has been escorted out of the room. Now, we need to discuss us." My heart stopped.

What did he want to talk about? I was terrified and steeled my heart, preparing it for a monumental rejection. Maybe having both of us there was too much? He was sweet with Arianna last night, but perhaps he realized it was something he didn't want after trying it out last night.

"Okay." I looked down to my fidgeting hands and chewed on my lip.

"I want you and Arianna to move in. I know you said it was too much and you couldn't but hear me out. If you want it to be a trial situation, that's fine with me. I'll have the guest room turned into a nursery, and you can have a room too. That way you'll have a place to get away if you need one. But I think you should move in this weekend, and we'll take it from there." He was almost babbling; he was so nervous.

Perhaps his worry didn't come from the enormity of what he was offering, but for the fact that I'd very likely say "no."

"Sinclair," I started, not sure how I was going to finish my thought. I wanted to move in, but it was all going too fast.

"If you say no," he added, "I want an impressively great

reason why it's not something we should at least try."

"Um, let's start with the fact that we just started dating on Monday, and it's Wednesday. And what reason is there for us to do this? You said yourself commitment wasn't your thing, so why are we even trying a micro-commitment situation that will inevitably end in my heartbreak?" And there it was.

We only had about nine minutes left of our drive, and I'd finally voiced my biggest fear… inevitable heartbreak.

"Well, let's go through the list of things I'll never do and assess where we are. One, I said I'd never date my assistant, well…" He looked over at me. "I hired you partially because I wanted to date you. Two, believe it or not, I've never had a one-night stand in costume. Three, I never planned on being a father. Four, I've never had a woman sleep over at my house… and five, I've never loved someone like I love you. If you think I'm not putting my heart on the line here, you're very wrong. This is scary for both of us, but I'm a go-getter, and I'm going to get this. We already have a kid; we're here Reyna… just jump with me." His sweet face was so convincing; I couldn't refuse.

"I'm probably making the biggest mistake in my life," I gave him a silly face, "but how can I not? I've already jumped."

"Then it's settled." He was beaming with delight when we pulled into the parking garage.

He parked the car in a private section reserved for executives. We decided I should go into the office before him and we'd switch it up daily, so it looked more realistic. We were playing with fire, but I didn't care. I was starting to love him too much to let this go.

Chapter 23

Sinclair

Reyna moved in that weekend. Lorna and Michael helped me decorate the nursery, with Reyna's approval. I initially offered her to take my credit card and decorate it herself. When I saw her on the Target website ordering a bunch of cheapo things, I stopped her and canceled her order. She didn't want her and Arianna to be an imposition on me, so she just ordered the cheapest. Crazy girl. She refused to spend my money, so I fired her from decorating. Since I loved decorating and creating amazing spaces, I took over the task and made a sanctuary for our little daughter. As for Reyna and her room, I didn't want to put too much effort into it. Selfishly, I hoped she'd spend her time in my room. I caught her looking at the Ikea website and shut her down from decorating her room as well.

"Seriously, Sinclair. You're being a control freak. Let me just order cheapo stuff."

I think she might have been sincerely pissed at me, but I didn't care. "No, no cheapo stuff in my house." I realized after I said it, I was wrong. Her glare proved it. "I mean, our house... it's our house now." Ugh, she got me. "So, what's your style?" I segued on our way home from work.

We only had a day to order everything and have it delivered. While I already had a bed in the other guest room, I wanted everything in the space to be hers.

"Bohemian artsy-fartsy," she finally conceded still slightly annoyed I was planning on spending much more money than she would have spent on the space.

I picked her some gorgeous handmade prints for her bed.
A local artist's artwork for the wall and little artsy-fartsy tidbits I
knew she would love. I was absolutely right; she adored the space.
It fit her style perfectly. By Sunday, they were all moved in. I think
she was still in shock, but I wasn't. The moment I closed the door
to the mansion and locked it, I felt safe and whole for the first
time since I was a child. I began to understand the phrase "you
complete me." I felt so complete and whole having them there.

Over the following week, Reyna came forward as one of
Christopher's victims, which, rumor had it, made him crazy angry.
We were settling into our lives together. The only challenge to
living with each other was trying to hide it from our co-workers,
and baby Arianna was a lot of work, yet worth every minute. I was
almost as in love with that beautiful baby girl as I was her mother.
I had to reorganize my time, making space for her schedule and
blocking out time to make love to her mother. Reyna and I also
needed to be alone to pursue our own dreams. Reyna had her
writing, and I had my company to run. All of it was hard work, but
for the first time in a long time, I felt truly alive.

We were cruising along fine until I came into work after
Reyna to find her talking with Ken.

"So what's the deal with you and Sinclair?" he whispered to
her after I walked into my office.

"Nothing… he's fine, just a little barky sometimes," she
dismissed.

"No, I'm not talking about what an ass he is. I mean,
what's up with you two hanging out with each other after work?
Molly saw you getting in his car after work last night," he said
pointedly. "And it isn't the first time. I'd be careful. Everyone
knows you've thrown your name into the hat with the Christopher
Regent thing. You might wanna be mindful of who you 'hang out

with.'" He used air quotes and laughed. "I mean if you want anyone to take you seriously, I suggest you not look like you're screwing your boss. I'm just being real with you."

"What the hell are you talking about?" she asked.

I wanted to come to her aid but wasn't exactly sure how.

"At least I know why you won't hang out with me. Do you do it for the money?" he pressed on being a complete fool.

"I'll have you know I didn't date you because you're an asshole, and this conversation proves it." She was fuming as she stood up and was about to leave, probably to cool down.

"Calm down, sweetie. I was just feeling you out. Seeing what my chances might be. But it looks like I was right. Christopher Regent and Sinclair have a lot more than hit movies in common. Alright girl, get your boss on… or off as the case may be; just watch your back. This #metoo thing is vicious."

"I'm not doing this," she said as she walked away.

After she left, it gave me the opportunity to confront Ken… a moment I'd been waiting for a long time. I exited my office and approached him, calm but menacing.

"I couldn't help overhearing your conversation with my assistant." He went as white as a ghost. "And… if I hear you talk to her in that kind of condescending manner ever again, I'll have you fired on the spot. In fact, I'm just going to Molly's office now to let her know as much. I don't care how good you think you are. If you talk to Reyna like that again, you're gone." I stared him dead in the eye.

He was shaken, but bold. "Is it true then? Are you and she being inappropriate? 'Cause if you are, I'm sure HR will have my back." He eyed me back with the same intensity I was giving him.

"You have no jurisdiction over my private affairs, so don't pretend you do." With that, I left him to talk with Molly.

She wasn't surprised to hear that her cocky assistant was being a dick, so she called him in to discuss the situation. When I met Molly later in the hall, she revisited the conversation saying Ken was adamant that Reyna and I had an affair. Molly mentioned she'd seen us together a few times as well. She kindly cautioned me to be careful. I knew Reyna and I will have to have to tell the company we were together. It was going to change a lot for us, but it was time. As much as I hated it, Molly and Ken were right. Our days as boss and assistant were numbered.

Later that day, Reyna and I had a legitimate reason to stay late at the office. We asked Lorna to pick up Arianna for us as we did a set visit for one of our movies. When we came back to the office, I was surprised to find my brother Shelton sitting in Reyna's chair.

"To what do I owe this unfortunate visit?" I confronted him, having had far too many run-ins with people I didn't like for the day.

"Just coming around to investigate the lawsuit against my client, little brother," he said, not making a move to leave Reyna's chair. "I've done a bit of digging, and it turns out your little assistant here has decided to accuse my client of sexual harassment."

"You're representing Christopher Regent. You can't talk to Reyna, it's illegal," I yelled nodding my head to Reyna to go into my office. "I'll take you home in a minute, as soon as I get this douche out of my face."

I was very on edge.

"Why are you telling your assistant you'll take her home?

Seems strange. Considering she's in a lawsuit against her previous boss for unwanted advances." He knew how to get me, and he was going for it. "If I had fucked Chris' assistant on Halloween night last year, then hired her out from under him I'd be very worried if he was still fucking her, even though I was her boss," the asshole threatened. "Especially, if I was hiding a secret love child. It could get really, really, messy. I don't judge. If you wanna stick your cock in every slut in Hollywood, be my guest. Just don't unleash her on Chris because we'll drag her through the dirt and find every man she's spread wide for."

He got me. I had a choice: continue to lie or face the truth and fight for Reyna and the others who had been so hurt by Christopher Regent.

"Trust me, Shelton, you don't want to go down this road. You'll end up being disbarred for intimidating a witness. I am not Chris. I don't have anyone claiming I've sexually harassed them, and as you're counsel for the defense, your being here can be considered intimidation." I was livid.

"I'm also your brother... so there's that." He was overly confident and unrelenting.

Hearing all of this, Reyna was a mess. She was sobbing when she passed us. I hadn't even thought to check on her; I was just so caught up in fighting with my brother.

"I called an Uber, Sinclair. Thanks for your offer, but I have a ride home." She left without saying anything else as she rushed out of the office.

My heart fell on the floor.

Chapter 24

Reyna

Why didn't he defend me? His brother called me a slut;
Ken pretty much did the same thing, and Sinclair… I was so
heartbroken. I wasn't really sure what he could do as we had to
keep our relationship a secret. But he could have fought for me,
for us. And yet, he couldn't, not if he wanted me to keep my job.
All I could do was cry. It was hard to keep my tears hidden from
Lorna when I picked Arianna up.

She was really confused as to why I was taking the baby,
but I just told her my roommates missed her, so we were going for
a visit. I couldn't think of a better lie on the spot. I was too
devastated. I think she suspected something was wrong. I had
been crying so much my eyes were red and puffy. I didn't care; I
just had to get Arianna and me out of there. I needed to breathe.

Everything had moved too fast. The nursery was more
beautiful than anything in a magazine; it was crazy over the top
and my room the same. Sinclair had bent over backward to
accommodate Arianna and me into his life. I loved living with him
even though he was overbearing at times, insisting he'd change
Arianna and choose what we eat, etc. It was all in the name of
love, but it was too much love. I needed air.

As soon as I opened the door to the apartment, Melody
and Charlynn freaked, but in a good way.

"Oh my God, finally you bring our baby back!" Melody
squealed as she grabbed for the baby. "Oh, hi, Reyna… we miss
you. It's too quiet here without you and Arianna."

"What happened? Did you forget some stuff? I thought

you were gonna leave some of your things here, you know, safety net and all ..." Charlynn stopped talking when she saw how red and painful my eyes looked. "Oh wait... you're falling, huh?"

That's all I needed; I burst into tears.

"OK, we're here," she said as she directed me to the couch.

"I don't think I can do this," I confessed through my tears.

"I knew he'd end up being a jerk, what did he do? I'll kill him," Melody said, rocking the baby in her arms.

"No. He's been great, too great. But this Chris thing... people are sniffing around, and pretty soon they're gonna find out about Sinclair and me and then... I just think we... I can't work for him and do this and us and..." I was babbling, I knew it, but my brain and emotions felt so scrambled.

"Okay. First, calm down. You haven't committed a crime. If you want to stay with him, you'll just have to get another gig. I'm sure he can help you. You don't love being an assistant. Maybe he'll help you sell one of your movies. He had you move in, so it's time you bring this thing out of the closet, girl." Charlynn held my hand.

"I know, but it might make things worse." I was so worried and confused; I felt like I'd fallen into an alternate universe. "Maybe I should pull out of the lawsuit against Chris."

"No, maybe you should just put on your big girl panties and deal with this. I know you got a lot going on Reyna, but you can handle it. We've got your back. I think down deep inside Sinclair is a solid dude; you just have to slow this train down a little. You don't know him. Just chill it out and do what normal people do. Date, hang out, text, then move in. I mean you guys are like bam, have a baby, bam work together, bam you're married. Chill it out some." Charlynn was giving me great advice.

The advice I didn't want to follow. At that moment, there was a knock at the door, and I nearly jumped out of my skin.

"I bet you a million dollars I know who that is," Melody said as she took the sleeping Arianna to my room.

Charlynn got up and opened the door. "What do you want to do? Do you want me to send him away, let him in, kick him in the nuts… where are we going from here?" Charlynn was so cool; I loved her.

"Let him in." My heart was still pooled on the floor, but it really wasn't his fault, he didn't do anything wrong.

I had high expectations for what I thought he should do, but I knew he couldn't do it. Charlynn opened the door to Sinclair standing there with a bouquet of flowers.

"Hi Charlynn, may I come in?" he asked, the perfect gentleman.

"Mi Casa es Su Casa," Charlynn said as she stepped aside to let Sinclair in.

He looked around the room to see Charlynn, Melody, and I looked back at him.

"These are for you." He handed me the flowers. "I know they don't make up for the horrible things that were said today, but at least they're pretty." He shrugged his shoulders. "Can we go someplace to talk?" he asked, being a businessman again.

"Thanks for the flowers. We can talk in my room."

We went to my room. I sat on the bed, and he walked over to Arianna's crib to see her sleeping.

"Lorna was so upset. She thought you were leaving us." He turned and looked at me. "I have to be honest; when she told me, I wasn't sure."

"We have to rethink this, Sinclair." I felt the tears welling in my eyes again as I choked that out. "I don't want there to be any repercussions for you. You don't deserve to be dragged into this. I'll just withdraw my charges and…" I couldn't hold them back, the tears just flowed.

He scooped me into his arms and held me tight. "We do have to rethink this, love. I agree. I want you to continue with the lawsuit against Christopher; he needs to be behind bars. I'm not going to get in the way of that. It's time we were honest about our relationship and our daughter. It probably means you getting a job at another company. I don't want that for you, and I don't think you want that for yourself either."

I stayed in his arms, quietly stunned.

"Hear me out before you say anything." He rubbed my arm, coaxing me to stay calm. "I'm going to give you some money to take care of the baby and focus on your writing. You can't come back to work, but this allows you time with Arianna and your dreams. I want you home with me, where you belong, but it's your choice. I just think we should lay low until Christopher is in prison.

"I love working with you, Sin," I protested.

"And I love working with you, but now you can do what you really want to be doing with your life. You barely have time to write, and when your little troll film goes into production, you need to focus on that. I haven't even heard you talk about your scripts for a while. I don't want you letting go of your dreams for me or anyone. This might be the best thing…"

I cut him off. "I don't want you to pay for me. I'm not a whore. I'm not a slut. I'm…"

"Of course you're not. And I'm certainly not paying a whore! I'm taking care of my family as a father should. It couldn't be more different."

"Is this what you really want?" I knew there was no way I was going to win this fight.

"No, but this is what we should be doing. This is ethical and right, and in the long run, I think it will be better for both of us." I was numb; I couldn't feel a thing.

He was punishing himself for this and in doing so also punishing me. I wasn't able to see it for what he was offering; a chance to raise my daughter and write movies. I saw it as being a kept woman who wouldn't have an independent income or any independence. It would be awesome to spend my day working on my scripts and pursuing my dreams, but I would resent him paying me… I was so stressed.

I sort of hoped he'd leave so I could sit with my feelings, but he stayed, ordered pizza and hung out with us. He spent the night with me, and we made love very quietly with him entering me from behind as we laid on my tiny bed. We practically laid on top of each other all night. At some point that night, he heard Melody get up and jam on her guitar. She had the door closed, but we could still hear it. I laughed and just told him she had trouble sleeping.

He was horny and wanted to have sex again but thought it was too crowded for a second round. I gave him a handjob under the sheets and giggled as he tried to stay quiet while he came in my hand. I rinsed off, cuddled in, and slept fitfully by his side, neither of us getting very comfortable. At some point, I must have dozed off because, by morning, he was gone.

Chapter 25

Sinclair

Even though I was doing the right thing, it sucked. After I left Reyna and Arianna and her delightful roommates, I had that familiar empty feeling again. I wanted her to come back to my home and live there. That's where they belonged. This hadn't changed anything at all. I had to remind myself we weren't doing anything wrong. I didn't want to get another assistant; I hated the idea. But I couldn't do the work alone, and sadly, if I kept Reyna, I'd violate work policy. A policy I demanded our company have to keep the employees safe.

Grace in human resources agreed I had to get another assistant. Given the climate in Hollywood these days, getting a new employee was advisable. I also added Arianna to my medical insurance and asked what concessions could be made for Reyna. Human Resources promised to offer Reyna a generous severance package and a year of medical insurance. That was good enough. I knew I'd take care of them for the rest of their lives, regardless.

"I'll get you a temp today, and we'll just move on. Hopefully, it'll all blow over." She flashed her plastic smile, and I felt sick.

I passed Ken's desk, and he looked small and sheepish. "Sorry about what I said about Reyna yesterday, Sinclair. It was really shitty."

I guess it was his attempt at an apology. "She quit. But since you seem so misinformed, I'll let you know the truth. We are in a serious relationship, and our daughter is loved and adored. So, if you ever insinuate that the mother of my child is a slut again, I'll have your nuts in a jar." I glared at him. "No one's job is secure these days. I'd watch my back if I were you," I threatened as I walked into my office and melted.

At the moment, life sucked. My temp arrived later that day, and she was attentive, perfect, plain, boring, unbearable. I didn't care. She did her job, and that's all I wanted her to do. I'd lost a little of my passion. I realized Reyna kept my spark alive. With her working by my side, I was on fire. I got projects off the ground, basked in the success of our Dark One franchise, and dreamed of our future.

It was then I remembered that she'd given me her scripts to read a few weeks back. She had her kid's troll project greenlit, but there were two more that hadn't been sold. I felt like I'd failed her by not reading them sooner. I decided to spend the day reading her scripts, and I was delighted to discover she was an incredible writer. What an imagination and so humble; she hadn't even said anything about how good she was. A lot of writers had an option on a script, yet they never got made. Her work was fantastic. I wanted all of them.

I knew I couldn't just greenlight a film without going through the proper channels even though it was my company. I had to bring them to the development meeting to be read by other execs. I put the scrips in the reading pile and redacted Reyna's name so people wouldn't think I was giving her preferential treatment.

By the end of the day, a tiny spark of life had returned. I was almost happy until my horrid brother Shelton came traipsing down the hall just as everyone was leaving.

"Hi, little brother. Where's your gorgeous assistant? I want to ask her some questions," he had the audacity to ask.

"It's still illegal to intimidate, threaten, or otherwise extract information from my assistant. She's a witness for the prosecution," I warned.

"I work for the firm representing Christopher Regent. I'm not his lawyer. Perhaps I'll represent her. I just have to see if she has a case." He was such a fucking a liar and not a very good one.

"She's sick. I sent her home, so you can go away now." I turned my back on him.

"Is she really worth it, Sinclair? She's an unwed mother. Chris says she came on to him and was relentlessly pursuing him and now she's fucking you. Do you really want to get messed up with someone like that?"

I thought about not doing it, but it must not have been long enough.

I turned back around and punched my brother in the face.

"What the fuck was that? I could have you on assault, brother, you better be careful." He held his nose, which was dripping blood. I felt triumphant.

"My relationship with my assistant is not your business. I'm not being accused of anything, and neither is she, so I suggest you get the fuck out of here before I call the police. You're at my place of business." I was livid.

"You know I'll find out what's going on, Sin. I will drag every woman you've ever dated into this. Get that bitch, slut assistant of yours to drop her case, or I'll come after you with everything I've got," the prick threatened.

"Go for it, Shel. You'll find absolutely nothing." I wasn't exactly sure he'd find nothing. I had a few women who hated me, but I never assaulted any of them. Every relationship I'd had was consensual.

He may have been able to find women who wanted revenge. Those might find his offer tempting, but I hoped not. For all my command and power, I was actually feeling very weak and unbalanced. The only person who could really help me out of my rut was my brother, Sage. I called him, as I often did in a crisis and told him I was coming over. I figured Reyna wouldn't come to my house without calling and sadly, she hadn't called or texted. I needed my younger brother's help... badly.

"So, okay. Let me understand. The amazingly hot dark angel girl you disappeared with on Halloween, showed up at your office to interview as your assistant, that's completely weird. AND... she had your baby, is now living in your house, and going after the biggest producer in Los Angeles for sexual harassment. You know how messed up this all sounds right?"

Well, if he put it like that, it sure did sound suspicious.

"I love her, Sage. Perhaps, instead of thinking of this as covert, you might see it as fate or serendipity." Of anyone in our family, he'd be the one to understand fate and serendipity.

"Have you had a paternity test? Do you know if the baby is really yours?" Who was this guy? My brother Sage was usually so cool and laid back.

"I don't have to; she looks like me," I defended.

"Like what? Squishy baby? Without a paternity test, you don't know for sure."

"What about trust? I believe her, and even if the baby isn't mine, I'd still raise her because that's what love does." I was livid. I came for advice, and I was getting a grilling from my little, guitar-playing brother who usually liked to chill and smoke weed with me.

194

What the hell was happening to my life?

"So is this it, Sinclair, this is the one?"

He got me. I had to think because he was right. Was this worth the fight? It would be different if I were just some guy, but I was Christopher Regent's closest rival. He was also being represented by my vindictive brother bent on causing me drama. Was Reyna worth putting everything in jeopardy with no guarantee of a happy ending?

"She is. I think this is it; she's the one." I couldn't believe I said it, but I was glad I did.

"Then fight for her. It might get really messy, but you got to bust this out into the open and put up the fight. If she's the one, then you have to come clean to the media and everyone about the baby and all of it. Otherwise, they will find out anyway and drag you both through the mud. Love hurts, buddy. If you love her, you gotta take a bullet for her."

"I love you, bro. You are so right."

I had to take it to the next level.

Playing house wasn't enough; I needed to make her a part of my world. My whole world.

Chapter 26

Reyna

I was staring at my phone. It'd become a habit. I didn't know why I kept picking it up; he hadn't called or texted all day. I thought perhaps he was busy at work without an assistant, and I was actually feeling sorry for him. It was well past the end of the day, and he hadn't even tried to reach me. I could've called him, but I wanted to know where he stood. He basically offered me money and just left this morning.

He said goodbye and was civil, but it was nothing like the passionate world we'd created for each other. I hated feeling like a whore or a slut because I was neither. Sinclair was it for me; he always had been.

"Stop looking at your phone, Rey. It only makes it worse," Charlynn scolded.

"I know. I know." I looked down at Arianna's sweet face and played with her tiny fingers. "I just thought he'd call by now."

"He's being a coward. As soon as there was a tiny bit of heat, he bailed. Such a man." Charlynn was pretty jaded. She didn't have the best luck with men, and most of them had treated her badly. Sadly, I was starting to believe she was right.

"I don't think he bailed, but…" I really didn't know what I thought, to be honest.

"You know you can always call him," Melody said, coming out of her bedroom with her guitar. "I have a new song; you guys gotta hear this. It'll take your mind off of jerkface."

I was happy to have a distraction.

"I don't want to seem pathetic, that's why I didn't call… Besides, if he's breaking up with me…" Those damn tears started to fall again, even though I was trying not to cry.

"Who spends a million dollars on shit for your room and then breaks up with you? I think you're being a little over-sensitive. He's probably just busy. You could've gone back to his house, that wouldn't have been desperate. So, tears deserve wine… buckets of wine. Play your song, Mel, and I'll get us some Pinot Noir."

I smiled, listening to Melody play her guitar as Charlynn brought us wine. I had the best friends on the planet, that's all I ever needed. Arianna and I would get through this. Sinclair had transferred two million dollars into my account that morning. I got a call from my bank saying a wire had come through from Sinclair Harris. I confirmed I knew him and was suddenly two million dollars richer. It should have been one of the best days of my life, but I felt completely awful.

"That was so great, Mel. I love that song." I burst into bigger tears. "I shouldn't have accepted the job," I sniffled, "I should've just left it all alone."

"But then you wouldn't have two million dollars. Hello? And some pretty amazing sex according to what little you told us," Charlynn reminded me.

"He was amazing, Char, it wasn't just the sex. He was so good with Arianna and…"

"Oh no, here she goes again," Melody interrupted, she handed me another tissue as mine was damp and crumpled.

Suddenly, we heard one of those crazy car horns, the ones that sound like a circus coming down the street.

"Oh my God, is it another Quinceanera? Or is it the time for prom? What time is it?" Charlynn was a little tipsy by that point.

I peeked out the window and saw a few black cars out there with dark tinted windows and a huge white stretch limousine between them. It must have been for a prom. Most likely, it was someone famous for making a scene. There were tons of paparazzi on the street. A thought crossed my mind—wouldn't it be funny if it were Sinclair, being grandiose? No planning, no true thought, just going balls out.

Just then, I got a text. *"Meet me outside your apartment. Put on a pretty dress and bring our daughter… we might end up in the news,"* with a smiley emoticon.

"Reyna, what's going on?" Charlynn asked after I got the text. I showed her my phone, and she laughed out loud. "That man is nuts."

"I knew it, it's Sinclair out there, isn't it? Holy shit…" Melody exclaimed.

I put on my prettiest dress and grabbed the baby. She was sleepy but sweet, and we all walked down to the street together. No way was I going to face this without the posse.

As we exited the apartment building together, Sinclair stepped out of the white stretch limo wearing a smokin' hot suit and carrying a bouquet of at least a hundred red roses. I was in total shock. He bent down on one knee, in the middle of the road with the paparazzi snapping away. Flashes went off all around us. I looked over to Charlynn and Melody, and they were as amazed as I was.

"Will you marry me? Sinclair asked, his beautiful emerald eyes looking up at me.

All I could do was nod my head, "yes."

"Let's switch, then." He stood up and handed me the bouquet of roses while he took Arianna into his arms.

"Oh shit. I forgot this." He fumbled, and for a moment, I thought he might drop Arianna as he stuffed his hand in his pocket and pulled out an enormous diamond ring. He didn't have a ring box or anything else, just a slick, big, blingy ring that he offered me. "Give me your hand," he said as he tried to wrangle the baby without waking her and put the massive ring on my finger.

Seriously, the ring was so big it would probably walk down the street before I did.

"Are you sure?" I whispered, looking at the gargantuan thing on my finger. "Is this really what you want?" I felt like we were filming an episode of some television drama.

"Yep," he answered without reservation. "This is what I've always wanted. Now get in the car so I can whisk you away."

I waved the ring at my roommates, and they went apeshit.

"We're riding off into the sunset. Don't wait up," he yelled to them as we got into the limo.

Once I was in the car, I saw Lorna and Michael sitting across from us. I was a little confused to see them. Most likely it meant Sinclair had more crazy up his sleeve.

"I know this is all a little soon and rushed…" Sinclair started as he handed Arianna to Lorna. "But it was the only way I could think of to dispel any rumors that might crop up."

My heart bottomed out. "Very clever," I said, trying to hide my disappointment. "Where did you get this ring?" I asked, taking it off. "It's insane." I handed the ring back to him "Make sure it gets back to wherever it came from; I'd hate to lose it." I was trying not to show my hurt.

He shook his head and took a deep breath. Lorna and Michael looked concerned as Sinclair calmly began to speak.

"Okay, I'm not sure if you've seen any romantic movies. I thought you had since you actually wrote quite a beautiful one. One, by the way, I've submitted to our development team for consideration. But... in case you missed it, I'll fill you in. I just proposed to you. As in 'will you marry me and live happily ever after kindathing. That ring is an engagement ring. A man gives a woman one when they want to spend the rest of their life with them."

He was being ridiculous.

"And... it was a publicity stunt so people will leave us alone. A publicity stunt is not the real thing," I said, correcting him as paparazzi flanked the car.

"Go ahead and drive to the office," he told the driver. "I don't want them taking pictures inside the car."

He then turned to me, handing me back the ring. "This wasn't a publicity stunt. I just asked you to marry me, legitimately. Now it can be a long engagement if you want. I'm impulsive, yet I can't think of anyone else in the world I want to marry. Take your time; we don't have to start wedding planning today. You do have to come back home to my house, so we can give this a shot. We owe each other the chance."

"Really?" I couldn't form any other words.

"Really. This way, we can explore our relationship and continue to fight Christopher. We are a united front; no one will pull us apart. If we choose to end it, it will be our own decision and not because of someone dragging our relationship out into the public arena. I love you. I want to spend my life with you… now all we have to do is get you to love me too." He flashed me a dashing smile.

"I do… I absolutely love you." I flung my arms at him as I watched relief dance across Lorna and Michael's faces.

"Good thing that went well." Lorna sighed. "I was worried there for a minute."

"Don't think you were any easier," Michael said in a dry monotone.

Chapter 27

Sinclair

I was thrilled that Reyna accepted my proposal. I knew she would, even if only out of shock. She needed time. I knew that, and in truth, I did too. Strangely, this was going to give us some space to continue to explore our relationship without people stalking and preying on us. The damn paparazzi followed the car all the way to the office as I thought they might. Everything was going to plan.

"The office is such a romantic place to celebrate our engagement." Reyna was being playfully snide. Her face still showed her confusion and shock, which was fine. Sarcasm was her way of dealing with things.

"Do you mind if Lorna and Michael keep Arianna for the weekend? We have a lot of your breast milk stored in the fridge; she'll have plenty. It's only if Momma can be away from her for a few days." I knew it was a lot to ask of her, so I was patient and expected a "no."

"She'd be no trouble for us; we'd love to have her," Lorna said, her eyes bright with expectation.

"It's going to be really hard, but as long as I can call every hour…" Reyna was very serious. "I think it'll be fine. We aren't going far, are we?" She looked at me and was a little fearful.

I had thought about whisking her away to Paris or some other romantic destination but decided there was no way she'd agree to be that far away from Arianna, so I settled for the next best thing.

"We'll be no more than an hour away should anything

happen. I'm taking a summer Friday off of work, and we're going away, but not that far away."

Luckily the garage doors closed just in time to block out the paparazzi. There were still a few on foot who tried to get pictures through the bars, but we turned a corner into the executive parking and lost them.

My publicist did a great job with this. She dropped hints to just the right people that there might be a story about one of the girls in the Christopher Regent case. She hinted I was involved so we'd get press. The paparazzi got hundreds of pictures of the proposal. Who'd accuse someone of sexually harassing a woman he intended to marry? The story for the papers was I met her at the Halloween party and got her away from Christopher. We fell in love, had a baby, worked together briefly, and were now getting married. It wasn't a perfect story, but this was Hollywood. People loved imperfect stories, especially if they were filled with drama.

I escorted Reyna out of the limousine, and she reluctantly left Arianna in Lorna's capable hands. I then shuttled her to the Westfalia, and her jaw dropped a few inches.

"What is this?" she marveled.

"My guilty pleasure. Hop in; I want to take you for a ride." I was beaming with joy.

The limo exited the parking garage, and the paparazzi went with them. A few lingered to see if we were pulling a bait and switch, so I opened the fridge in Westy and pulled out a bottle of champagne and two glasses. I had a tray of snacks as well… all of Reyna's favorites.

"I thought we might wait out the paps for a bit. I brought snacks." I poured a glass of champagne and handed it to her. "To impulsive marriage proposals."

"To insane people." She raised her glass to meet mine.

We drank our champagne, ate the snacks, and made out in the back of the Westy for about an hour before I felt the coast was clear.

"I think we lost them. Time for my surprise." I felt giddy for the first time in forever.

"Wasn't the wedding proposal thing surprise enough?" Her eyes were wide and questioning.

"Nope." I couldn't stop smiling.

"Okay," she looked at me, suspiciously. "It's not a scary surprise right; you know how much I love those." Ah, the sarcasm again.

"I hope not," was all I gave her.

It was about a forty-five-minute drive to my beach house in Malibu. My parents gave each of their sons a house. Shelton lived in his three-bedroom loft on the top floor of a live/work space in downtown. Sage rented his mansion in Brentwood out for an enormous sum, so he could pursue his music. He lived, rent-free, in a little studio apartment in a collection of apartments my parents owned. I was just babysitting the mansion for my parents. They gave me the smallest of their dwellings, a tiny beachside bungalow in Malibu since we all assumed the mansion would someday be mine.

It wasn't that tiny. It had a living room facing the ocean, a loft, and two bedrooms. It was, in a word, paradise. I thought Reyna might enjoy being there to celebrate this momentous occasion because she always thought the mansion was too big and elegant for "normal" people to live in. The beach house would be more to her liking.

We stopped at In-n-Out Burger before we arrived because I knew there wouldn't be any food at the house. I'd go out to the neighborhood market in the morning. I knew Reyna would love the fact that there was no chef and no servants to wait on us. We were just going to be regular people doing regular things… in paradise.

I loved the delighted expression on her face when she saw the beach house. She rushed into my arms, hugged my neck, and kissed me.

"This place is absolutely amazing," she gushed and twirled.

"This is all ours," I said, returning her enthusiasm. "…and only ours."

It was a little too Sound of Music for me, but she was adorable. I never thought of this tiny house on the water as being "absolutely amazing." I looked around the room trying to see it through her eyes, and I understood the fascination. The window facing the ocean was two stories tall. The ocean view was completely unobstructed. Wherever we were in the house, we could see the water.

The bungalow had a loft over the living room and kitchen, two small bedrooms, and a terrace right on the sand. We had some chairs and a fire pit out there, but in all the bungalow was fairly quaint by Harris family standards. It was part of a private community of houses that shared a secluded beach. Most of the people living there were retirees; we were virtually alone that night. We ate our In-n-Out burgers on the terrace. She had a grilled cheese and me a double-double. It was fun listening to the ocean lap against the sand as we drank champagne and ate cheap burgers.

"Are you sure you really want to do this?" she asked again.

"I'm never truly sure of anything, but I want us to try," I answered. "Are you sure you want to do this?" I didn't know if I wanted to hear her answer, but honesty was always the best policy.

"I'm terrified, Sinclair. Not of loving you, but I... I just don't want to be hurt." Her gaze lowered. "I've only been with one man before you, and he broke up with me in a rather harsh way. I don't entirely trust men." Her eyes lifted to mine after her confession.

"You shouldn't trust men, but you should trust me," I assured her as I took her hand. "I'm in this for the long term. I love you, Reyna. As long as we give each other space, be truthful with our feelings, and communicate, I think we can make this work. We haven't known each other that long, but I already know I don't want to be with anyone else. I am going to make love to you tonight and for as many nights as I can, proving to you every day that I love you."

Her smile was warm and resolved. "I love you," was all she said.

I picked her up and carried her into the bedroom and sat her on the bed. I then undressed and bared myself, naked and erect. She did the same. I was not hers, and she was not mine; we belonged to each other... equals.

She softly dipped to her knees and took my cock into her mouth, lovingly sucking on my most tender organ. I let her dictate the seduction that night. I didn't thrust into her mouth but rather enjoyed the sensations of her soft, warm wetness on my tender skin. Her hands captured my buttocks and dove me deeper in as my balls tickled and clenched. I took deep breaths to make sure I didn't cum in her mouth. I wanted the evening to last. Her tongue flicked at my swollen slit as her hand stroked up and down until I was clenching my teeth and sucking in air to hold back my release.

I was so close to climax as I always was in her mouth. I gently pulled myself out.

"I'm good, love," I said as I lifted her from the floor and kissed her mouth, tasting me on her lips.

I pressed her gently to the bed. "I love you," I said as my hand slid down her body, dancing around her nipples and the sides of her perfect hourglass figure until it found purchase in her sweet wet center. I enjoyed diving my finger in and out of her, making sure to rub and flick her clit intermittently as I sucked her breasts.

Her fingers entwined in my hair, "Oh, Sin... oh my God," she cried when I dove three fingers in her and pressed my body weight into them.

The thumb rubbed her clit, and I heard the glorious sounds of her climax. My mouth returned to hers as she came and captured my lower lip between her teeth. I grabbed her leg and draped it over my belly and dove myself into her exquisitely beautiful body. I held her steady as I began languidly pulsing, kissing her breasts, her shoulders, her neck...

She bit my earlobe. It was surprising and made me thrust harder involuntarily. Her hand wrapped around my back as she shifted on top of me. "You feel so good." Her eyes glazed over and became hazy.

I adored her dazed look of euphoria. I always knew it meant she was close to orgasm again.

She started riding me hard, driving me nuts. I wasn't going to last much longer.

"Sin... Sin," she blathered as another wave of ecstasy hit her.

It was all I could take. I rolled on top of her, spreading her wide as I rocked into her deeper and deeper until our bodies were melded as one. Her hot skin slicked to mine, being skin to skin, body to body was too much. I felt my balls tightening as her pussy sucked at me, and she arched forward as she screamed my name.

I buried my cock as deep as I could and released my load, shooting stream after stream of cum into her womb. We had one glorious baby, but I had a primal need for more. Whenever I was with Reyna, my body just wanted to make her pregnant over and over again.

My head, of course, knew how wrong this was, but boy my body sure as shit didn't care. Good thing she was taking the pill, or we'd be up to our ears in kiddos. Coming down from my orgasm, I laid beside her and stared at the beautiful breezy expression on her face.

"Do you know one of the things I love most about being engaged to you?" I asked, hazy with my own euphoria.

"What's that?" She turned to me and propped her head on her hand, staring with so much love.

"I get to do this with you for the rest of my life." I kissed her again and finally pulled my cock out of her pussy, sated and tired.

"And I get to too," she cooed, her finger swirling on my pubic hair, tracing the lines of the tattoo angled towards my manhood which had the nerve to semi-inflate again.

"I have a crazy idea," I blurted out.

"What's that?" she asked, intrigued.

"Let's walk on the beach naked and make love on the sand." I was being so crazy.

"You sure Ethel and Wilma will be good with that? This is a retirement community after all," she teased.

"It's a private community full of mostly retirees; there's a difference. But I don't think Ethel nor Wilma will mind. Perhaps they'll get inspired and do a little muff diving themselves." I winked at her.

"Oh my God, you're horrible. Let's go—I wanna ride your waves, baby." She was being so cute and cheesy.

"Do me a favor and never use that as a line in one of your movies ever, just don't," I said as I took her hand and walked out to the beach with her.

Life continued around us as we made love in the surf that night. We were simply specs before the vastness of the ocean. In our world, though, the one where it was just our little family, we sparked a fire that night. It was a never-ending blaze that would illuminate us the rest of our lives.

Sarah J. Brooks

Epilogue

Reyna

We had a lavish wedding in Malibu. I was reluctant to plan anything big, and I didn't necessarily want to rush into marriage, but after our weekend at the Malibu house, I changed my mind. Sinclair, away from the world and the way the world saw him, was the perfect human. I loved him with all my heart. He was already the father of my daughter, and so I embraced our future together. We had a year-long engagement. Arianna and I moved into Sinclair's mansion for good after that weekend in Malibu. Not much changed after we were married, other than we shared a last name and a very sizable bank account.

Our family had a rather busy life, but we managed it well. Ariana would go to Mrs.Effleman on weekdays, while Sinclair went to the office and I worked on my many film projects. Lorna offered to help with Arianna a lot at night, and I let her on occasion when Sinclair had something romantic planned for us, but usually, we wanted to take care of her ourselves after being away from her all day.

My parents had never really been a big part of my life, but I did let them know I was planning on getting married. They seemed surprised but happy I was marrying a billionaire. Strange, but I'd never really thought about his money. We were a team; we worked hard and continued to grow our wealth. We didn't horde it but funded projects with important messages and gave back to our community whenever we could.

His production company produced two of my scripts,

and the little troll project was a very successful children's film. I was working a lot, and I loved it. I would often cart us all off to Malibu to write on the weekends. I found it more inspiring, and Sinclair was much less tense there. Our lovemaking was always just a little better in that magical place.

I loved waking up to the sound of the surf and dolphins playing in the waves. A year after our wedding, I was pregnant again. I loved being a mother, and we decided we wanted a few children and spread them out over a few years, so we could still work. Sinclair and I both loved parenting and felt most rewarded when we were with our family. Neither of our parents had much presence in our lives, so we vowed to be more present and available for our own children. I was thrilled to be bringing new life into the world.

Although our lives together are action-packed, Sinclair and I have been happy every day. We are perfect for one another. We're good friends first, lovers second, and parents always. We knew we could conquer the world… and we did … one little film at a time. We made movies that mattered, helped bring Christopher Regent to his knees and were raising children to be kind, thoughtful citizens of the planet Earth. Sinclair was right… we did end up having a happily ever after.

Sinclair

A year after our wedding we found out Reyna was pregnant with Sinclair junior. Arianna was three years old and was excited to have a little brother. I never expected to be a father, but I sure loved it. After a little more than two years, the lawsuit with Christopher Regent finally went to court. Fifty-seven women came forward, and in the end, Chris was convicted on all counts. He will be spending the rest of his life in prison. Reyna and I were both relieved when it was all finally over. She was so brave and strong through the whole ordeal. Now, he couldn't hurt anyone anymore.

The Dark One franchise took off. The second installment had the highest box office for the opening weekend, and Reyna and I were prepping for the premiere of The Dark One Three, The Legacy. I was so proud that we'd hired Reyna to write the script for the third installment of the Dark One franchise. I knew it was our best one yet. We were going to premiere it on Halloween night... which I found ironic.

We had Sage and Rey's roommates over to the house a lot. We loved to barbecue and entertain. We had the Dark One premiere on Halloween at sunset, but before that, we hosted a kids' party at the Mansion. Reyna, Arianna, and I were dark angels. Arianna was so cute with her gorgeous blonde curls against the dark black of her costume. She was turning out to be just like her mother, strong, funny, and in control; we were merely at her service. I loved her desperately. Sinclair Jr. had more of Reyna's dark coloring. He had her chocolate brown eyes and deep brown curls; he had my strong profile, though. I had to admit we made gorgeous children. I never really thought I'd ever been this happy. I knew I'd make movies and probably would end up being a success… but nothing like this. I married my best friend and the perfect companion for the happily ever after. I guess if I were to muse on it, I'd say sometimes the only thing we need to make our lives perfect, is to believe that a perfect life exists.

THE END

Dear reader,

thank you so much for reading my book, it really means the world to me! If you liked it and want to do me a little favor, please leave a short review on Amazon – that would be too wonderful!

XOXO
Sarah

Made in the USA
Coppell, TX
25 November 2019

11869010R00125